ENCHANTMENT

ENCHANTMENT

*Fairy Tales, Ghost Stories
and Tales of Wonder*

Kevin Crossley-Holland
Illustrated by Emma Chichester Clark

Orion
Children's Books

First published in 2000
by Orion Children's Books
a division of the Orion Publishing Group Ltd
Orion House
5 Upper Saint Martin's Lane
London WC2H 9EA

These stories first appeared in *British Folk Tales* by Kevin Crossley-Holland,
published by Orchard Books in 1987. The versions of Tom Tit Tot, Samuel's Ghost
and The Dauntless Girl reproduced in this book were first published
by Colt Books in *The Old Stories*, 1997.

Typeset at The Spartan Press Ltd
Lymington, Hants
Printed in Italy by Printer Trento S.r.l.

for Gillian,
Kieran and Dominic,
Œnone and Eleanor

✦ CONTENTS ✦

THE COW THAT ATE THE PIPER   *8*

FAIRY OINTMENT   *12*

THE FROG PRINCE   *18*

THE SHEPHERD'S TALE   *21*

TOM TIT TOT   *24*

BILLY   *32*

THREE HEADS OF THE WELL   *35*

HUGHBO   *44*

MONDAY, TUESDAY   *49*

SAMUEL'S GHOST   *58*

THE CHANGELING   62

MOSSYCOAT   66

KING OF THE CATS   80

DATHERA DAD   83

SEA-WOMAN   85

CHARGER   91

THE THREE BLOWS   93

THE MULE   106

THE DAUNTLESS GIRL   117

BOO!   126

SOURCES OF THE TALES   127

THE COW THAT ATE THE PIPER

The three hired men left the farm on a cold November morning. They slung their sacks over their shoulders and set out on the long walk back home to Kerry.

That evening, the moon shone and the north wind pursed his blue lips and whistled. And the three men couldn't see so much as a haystack, let alone an old barn, to shelter and sleep in. They quickened their pace, they trotted, they sang, they swung their arms, and before long they fell into step with a laughing piper. He was bare-footed and wearing no more than a tatter of clothing.

"I'll go along with you," said the piper.

The frost tightened his white fist: bushes by the roadside hunched their shoulders; the road began to glitter.

"We're all dead men," said the piper, "if we don't keep moving."

The four of them kept walking, trotting, walking and shortly before midnight, they came across a dead man lying right across the road. He was wearing a brand-new pair of shoes.

"Faith!" said the piper. "Look at those shoes!"

The three men looked and the moon polished the shining toecaps.

"I haven't so much as a stitch on my feet," said the piper. "They're no use to him, are they now?"

"Not at all!" said one of the hired men.

"I'll take them off of him," said the piper. He got down on all fours and tugged at the dead man's shoes. But he could do no more than untie the laces.

"Death alive!" exclaimed the piper. "They're frozen to his feet!"

"Come on now," said another of the hired labourers. "We're decent men."

"Give me your spade!" the piper said. "Let's see if I can't cut off his legs."

So the piper cut off the dead man's feet at the ankles. He picked them up and popped them into his sack. Then he and the hired men hurried on and just after midnight, they came upon a little farm.

"Heaven be praised!" said the piper.

The men knocked, they waited, knocked again and after rather a long time a sleepy serving-girl unbolted the door and let them into the kitchen – a low-slung smoky room with the fire at one end and three cows tied up at the other.

"You can sleep here," said the girl. "But keep clear of that grey cow. She's a devil. She'll eat the coats off of your backs." The girl latched the door at the foot of the stairs, and padded up to her own room.

Before long, the three hired men curled up round the burning peats and fell asleep. The piper, though, still had work to do. He opened his sack and took out the shoes with the two feet inside them, and toasted them over the fire. The feet began to thaw and he was soon able to pull off the shoes.

The piper smiled. He drummed his fingers on the shining toecaps and hummed a little tune. Then he put his own feet into the shoes! He stood up; he hopped and spun around; and he threw the dead man's feet down the far end of the kitchen.

For a while the piper dozed. Then at dawn, while the household and the hired men were still asleep, he got up, shouldered his pipes and his sack, and crept out of the house.

The serving-girl was first to rise. She came downstairs, and roused the huddle of sleepers. The three hired men groaned and rubbed their eyes and sat up.

"There were four of you at midnight," said the girl.

The men yawned and ran their hands through their hair.

"Where's the one with the pipes?"

"I don't know," said the first man.

"How should we know?" said the second man. And the third man just shrugged. The girl walked down to the far end of the kitchen and there she stumbled right over the two feet.

"Holy mother!" she cried. "The cow has eaten him!"

The serving-girl ran to the foot of the staircase. "The cow!" she yelled. "The grey cow! The cow has eaten the piper!"

"What's that?" shouted the farmer, and he stumped down the stairs, a great rumple-and-crease of a man.

"The cow's eaten the piper!" shouted the girl. "The poor cold piper! There's only his feet left."

The big pink farmer looked at the feet. He looked at the hired men and the men advanced to the middle of the room.

"There were four last night then," he said.

"There were," said the first man.

"And our comrade," said the second, "he's been eaten by that grey cow."

The farmer looked around him, as if the walls themselves had ears. "Shush!" he said, and he put a stubby finger to his lips. "No need for any trouble now."

Then the farmer dipped into his clothing and fished out five gold coins. "Here's five guineas for you," he said, pressing the coins into the palm of the first hired man. "Now eat your breakfast and be off."

As soon as they had eaten breakfast, and it was not a small one, the three hired men shouldered their sacks and left the little farm.

Some way down the winding road, they caught up with a laughing man wearing no more than a tatter of clothing. The golden sun polished his toecaps and he was hopping and spinning and dancing a jig.

FAIRY OINTMENT

Febuary and freezing. In sunlight and starlight the wind blew from the east. It gripped the land. It poked its fingers under doors and through squints and along passageways.

Joan sat by the fire, and saw faces in it, and journeys and destinations. Joan rubbed her dry lips against each other. Slowly she shook her head.

"An old woman," she said, "sitting in her bone-house. I grow old dreaming of all the things that never happened."

The wind gave tongue to the elm and the oak, the creaking house, and the taciturn stones: the night was so full of voices that at first Joan did not hear the knocking at her door.

The noise grew sharper: bare knuckle against wood. Joan stirred. "Of all nights," she said.

She unbolted the door and then the wind swung it wide open and threw in her visitor. He was small and dark like most of the hill-farmers, and he was cross-eyed.

"Well," said Joan, forcing the door back into its frame, "what's blown you in?"

"It's my wife," said the man. "She's gone into labour. Can you come up and help?"

"Up where?" said Joan.

"Up the back," said the man. "Up past the old fishpond. I've brought a horse."

"I see," said Joan.

"That's not her first, mind," said the man.

So Joan parcelled herself inside warm

wrappings: gloves and a hood and scarves and leggings and a cloak that
was really an old blanket with two holes cut in it for the arms.

Then the little man mounted his black horse and Joan mounted behind
him. The sky's pane was incised with sparkling stars and a full moon; the
earth's locked doors were covered with patches of snow. Joan buried her
face in her cloak and they rode over the hill at the back, past the blind eye
of the fishpond, and up towards the mountain.

No sooner had the little man and Joan galloped into the farm courtyard
than a door was thrown open and a young girl ran out calling, "Father!
It's a boy! It's a boy!"

Inside the house, Joan was surrounded by a swarm of children. They
followed her out of the big friendly kitchen, chattering and laughing.
They followed her down the cold passage and up the stone stairs.

"Shush!" said Joan, rounding on them, and wagging her finger at them.
"She can do without that."

The little man led Joan into a hushed bedroom and all the children
trooped in after her. The room was lit with candles, at least twenty of
them, and the man's wife was lying pale on the bed. Her tiny baby was
tucked against her.

"He couldn't wait," said the woman. "The little imp!"

"Now then!" said Joan. Firm and friendly, she pressed her palm against the woman's brow, and plumped her pillows, and then picked up the little baby. He was fast asleep. "Welcome!" said Joan. "Welcome to this wide world!"

The woman raised herself on one elbow and fished in the little cupboard beside her bed. "No need to wake him," she said. "But when he does wake up, will you smear this ointment on his eyelids?"

Joan took the ointment and shook her head. "Whatever you say," she said.

"And be careful," said the little man, "not to get any on your own eyes."

"All right!" said Joan. "Do we need all these children in here?"

The little man shooed some of his children out of the room, but it didn't seem to do much good. It only made more space for those who were left to wrestle and skip and squabble, and before long, those that went out at the door came in at the window.

Joan washed the baby and still he slept; the little man busied himself downstairs; the woman drowsed after her labour.

Then the baby opened his eyes and Joan saw at once that he had a bit of a squint, just like his father. "Ah me!" she said, and she shook her head and sighed.

Then Joan picked up the little box of ointment. *Anyway*, she wondered, *what's it for*? She opened it, dabbed at it with her little finger, and smeared a little on to each of the baby's eyelids. Then Joan glanced quickly and sideways at the baby's mother, and smeared a little of the ointment on her own right eyelid.

Joan blinked and opened her eyes. With her left she saw no different – the squinting baby on her lap, wound and wrapped in an old white shawl; his sleeping mother in the sagging bedstead; the scruffy children; the simple and homely farm furniture. But with her right eye, Joan saw that she was sitting in an airy and elegant room, surrounded by precious antique furniture. The baby on her lap was wrapped and wound in gauze flecked with silver and looked more beautiful than before; and his sleeping mother was robed in white silk.

The children in the room, however, looked even less wholesome than they had done before. They were imps with squashed noses and pointed ears. They pulled faces at each other, and scratched their heads like monkeys, and with their hairy paws they picked and plucked their mother's bedclothing, and pulled her ears.

Joan looked and looked. She looked and said nothing.

Before dawn, Joan had finished all her midwife's work. She had washed the baby as clean as a cat's tongue; she had made his mother's bed; she had driven the children out of the room for the seventeenth time; she had put the baby to his mother's breast where he had fed and promptly fallen asleep again. There was nothing more for her to do.

"Take me home now!" Joan said to the little man. She sounded confident enough but she was shaking. She glanced round the beautiful room; she looked at the little man, dressed in velvet, and squinting. "East, west," she said, "home is best."

Joan needn't have worried. The little man was delighted at the way in which the midwife had looked after his wife and their new baby. He brought his coal-black horse round to the door; and now Joan saw that its eyes were fiery red.

Away they went, into the crystal night, through the burning icy wind. They galloped past the old fishpond, and down to Joan's little cottage at the foot of the hill. There, the little man helped Joan dismount. He thanked her and gave her a gold coin for her night's work. Joan unbolted her door and, safely inside, tested the coin between her teeth. Then she threw some wood on the fire and lay down in front of it. She closed one eye; she closed the other, and she fell asleep.

A few days later, Joan picked her way along icy lanes into the nearby town. It was market-day and she needed meat and vegetables; she wanted some company.

In the market, Joan was amongst friends. She had known most of the people there, buyers and sellers alike, for as long as she could remember. So the morning was taken up with a pleasant mixture of business and talk.

While she stood gossiping at one stall, Joan saw something out of the corner of her right eye: a little man, just a couple of feet away, had picked up an apple and, without paying for it, slipped it into his canvas bag.

Joan frowned and watched more carefully as the man sauntered down to the next stall. There, he took two leeks and quickly dropped them into his bag too.

"You!" called Joan. "What do you think you're doing?"

The little dark man whirled round to face her.

"It's you," said Joan, astonished and fearful.

"Good morning, Joan," said the little man.

What Joan had meant to say stayed inside her mouth. "How's your wife?" she stammered. "The baby?"

"You can see me then," said the little man.

Joan nodded.

"Which eye, Joan?" asked the little man, smiling.

Joan covered her left eye. She covered her right eye. "This one," she said.

The little dark man raised a hand and lightning flashed in Joan's right eye, a searing dazzle and then shooting stars and then complete darkness.

"That's for meddling!" cried the little man. "That's for taking the ointment, Joan! You won't be seeing me again."

Joan never saw anyone again, not with her right eye. She was blind on that side until the day she died.

THE FROG PRINCE

It was high and dry summer. The tall nettles behind the widow's cottage swayed and looked sorry for themselves. A silly warm wind chafed the elder leaves and the long grass.

The widow was making barley-cakes and realised she had too little water.

"We're out," she said to her daughter. "And I only need a thimbleful more."

"I'll go," said Jessie. "We'll be needing some later."

It was quite a walk through the hamlet and across the meadow, and when Jessie reached the well she found it was dry. There was not a drop of water in it.

Jessie sat down on the well's coping, feeling quite worn out. *I can't go back*, she thought, *not without some water. And there* is *no water…* Two tears slowly gathered in the corners of her eyes and, without knowing quite why, she began to weep.

Then a frog came leap-leap-leaping out of the well. He hopped round the coping and looked up at Jessie. "What's wrong?" he said. "Lassie!" he said. "What are you crying for?"

"It's dry," sobbed Jessie. "There's no w-w-"

"Wipe your eyes!" said the frog. "If you'll marry me, I'll give you plenty of water."

Jessie wiped her eyes and smiled at the frog.

"You heard," said the frog.

Jessie didn't think the frog could be serious.

"Marry you!" she said. "Yes, of course I'll marry you!"

The frog took Jessie's earthenware jug and disappeared into the well. Two minutes later he was back and the jug was brimming with water.

Jessie shook her head and took the jug. "Thank you," she said. "Thank you very much."

The girl hurried home and her mother made the barley-cakes; and that night, just as they were about to go to bed, they heard something moving outside the door, and then they heard this song:

> "Oh! open the door, my honey, my heart;
> Open the door, my own true love.
> Remember the promise you and I made
> Down in the meadow, where we two met."

"What's that?" said the widow. "What's that song at the door?"

"Tut!" said Jessie, wrinkling up her pretty nose. "It's nothing but a filthy frog."

"Open the door for the poor frog," said the widow.

So Jessie opened the door and the frog came leap-leap-leaping in. He crossed the floor and sat down by the hearth. Then he sang:

> "Oh! give me my supper, my honey, my heart;
> Give me my supper, my own true love.
> Remember the promise you and I made
> Down in the meadow, where we two met."

"Tut!" said Jessie. "As if I would give supper to a filthy frog."

"Oh yes!" said the widow. "You must give the poor frog his supper."

So the frog got his supper and when he had finished it he sang again:

"Oh! take me to bed, my honey, my heart;
Take me to bed, my own true love.
Remember the promise you and I made
Down in the meadow, where we two met."

"Tut!" cried Jessie. "Would I ever take a filthy frog to bed?"

"Oh yes!" said the widow. "If that's what you promised, that's what you must do. Take the poor frog to bed."

So Jessie took the frog into her bed, and then he sang again:

"Now fetch me an axe, my honey, my heart;
Fetch me an axe, my own true love.
Remember the promise you and I made
Down in the meadow, where we two met."

Jessie went off to fetch an axe, and then the frog sang once more:

"Now chop off my head, my honey, my heart;
Chop off my head, my own true love.
Remember the promise you and I made
Down in the meadow, where we two met."

Well, Jessie chopped off the frog's head. And no sooner had she done so than up started the most handsome prince in the world. The prince married Jessie and the two of them were happy for as long as they lived.

THE SHEPHERD'S TALE

That's where I saw them! Up on that green patch there…

That's fifty years, see. I was missing one ewe and high up and calling. First there was such a winking and glittering. Then I saw them quite clearly – little men and women dancing in a ring.

I'll tell you then. I hurried towards them and first thing caught my eye – they were wearing scarlet or white, every one of them. Scarlet or white. A kind of uniform, see. The men had tripled caps on their heads and the women, they wore white lacy kinds of things. Fantastical! They waved in the wind.

My! Those ladies were lovely! I've seen some beauties, mind, some rare beauties. The men, too, they were handsome.

There were three harpists there, sitting on flat stones and playing for the dancers. Plucking and rippling! The strange thing is I couldn't hear a note. I saw them playing but they didn't make a sound.

Round and round whirled the dancers, smiling and laughing. And when they spied me, they nodded and smiled, and some of them threw up their arms and beckoned me. Then they all joined hands again. Faster and faster, leaning backward, almost falling! Laughing faces!

There were others, too, mind. Little men running races, sprinting and scurrying, and others clambering over the old cromlech – up one side, along the top, and down the other. That's as old as Adam, that. Prehistorical! Not so long back, two men came all the way from Cardiff just to measure it…

Where was I then? Yes, and horses. There were ladies riding round on dapper white horses. Side-saddle, mind. Nothing wanton! Their dresses were white – white as misty sunlight and red as young blood.

Well, then, I'll tell you. I came close and very close. I stuck out one foot, just into the ring. I heard it then, the fairy music. Harps, what a sound, yes! My heart started jigging. There's a sound a man could die for.

So I stepped right into the ring, see. At once I saw I was in some kind of palace. The walls were covered with gold and pearls.

One young woman walked up to me. "Come with me, Dai!" That's what she said. "We've been expecting you."

Then she showed me round – all the shining rooms, and the coloured gardens.

"You can go where you want, Dai," she said.  "There's just one thing…"

"What's that?" I said.

"You see this well?"

I looked into the well and it was teeming with fish, see. Red and blue and black and green. And some of them were gold.

"You see this well?" she said. "Whatever you do, Dai, never drink a drop."

The young woman led me back through the palace to a feasting-hall. There was venison and lamb and sucking-pig; pheasant and grouse and pigeon. All of it carried in on silver platters, mind. And you know who carried it? Beautiful ladies! That was a place, all right!

And there was red wine and yellow wine, I remember that. I drank them both, see. I drank them from gold goblets covered with diamonds and rubies and emeralds. Strong wine and sweet wine! Before then, I'd only tasted water and milk and beer.

Whatever I wanted, they brought it to me. Food, drink, warm water to wash with, a comfortable bed. I wanted harpists, singers, acrobats! Then I wanted to talk to their little children. A whole troop came in, chattering and giggling. They were small as dandelions.

You know what I wanted most? It's always the same, mind. You want what you can't have. That's the old Adam.

After dark, I sneaked out into the garden, see. I ran down to the well. Then I plunged in this hand – and all the coloured fishes, they disappeared. Then I cupped my hands and lowered them into the water…

Oh! What a shriek there was! Glassy and piercing, like the moon in pain. A shriek right round the garden and the palace.

Never mind, I closed my eyes and sipped the water!

The garden and the palace and the little people inside it, they all dissolved. In front of my eyes they just dissolved. Mountain mist.

It was dark, hopeless dark, and I was standing alone on the side of the mountain. Up there, that green patch, see. Standing right in the place where I stepped into the ring.

TOM TIT TOT

There was once a little old village where a woman lived with her giddy daughter. The daughter was just sixteen, and sweet as honeysuckle.

One fine morning, the woman made five meat pies and put them in the oven. But then a neighbour called round and they were soon so busy gossiping that the woman forgot about the pies. By the time she took them out of the oven, their crusts were as hard as the bark of her old oak tree.

"Daughter," she says, "you put them there pies in the larder."

"My! I'm that hungry," says the girl.

"Leave them there and they'll come again," says the woman. And what she meant, you know, was that the crusts would get soft.

"Well!" the girl says to herself, "if they'll come again, I'll eat these ones now." And so she set to work and ate them all, first and last.

When it was supper time, the woman felt very hungry.

"I could just do with one of them there pies," she says. "Go and get one off the shelf. They'll have come again by now."

The girl went and looked, but there was nothing on the shelf except an empty dish. "No!" she calls. "They haven't."

"Not none of them?" says the woman.

"No!" calls the girl. "No! Not none."

"Well!" says the woman. "Come again or not, I'll have one for my supper."

"You can't if they haven't come," says the girl.

"I can though," says the woman. "Go and get the best one."

"Best or worst," says the girl, "I've eaten the lot, so you can't have one until it's come again."

The woman was furious. "Eaten the lot? You dardle-dumdue!"

The woman carried her spinning wheel over to the door and to calm herself, she began to spin. As she spun she sang:

"My daughter's ate five; five pies today.
My daughter's ate five; five pies today."

The king came walking down the street and heard the woman.

"What were those words, woman?" he says. "What were you singing?"

The woman felt ashamed of her daughter's greed. "Well!" she says, beginning to spin again:

"My daughter's spun five; five skeins today.
My daughter's spun five; five skeins today."

"Stars of mine!" exclaims the king. "I've never heard of anyone who could do that." The king raised his eyebrows and looked at the girl, so sweet and giddy and sixteen.

"Five today," says the woman.

"Look here!" says the king. "I want a wife and I'll marry your daughter. For eleven months of the year," he says, "she can eat as much food as she likes, and buy all the dresses she wants; she can keep whatever company she wishes. But during the last month of the year, she'll have to spin five skeins every day; and if she doesn't, I'll cut off her head."

"All right!" says the woman. "That's all right, isn't it, daughter?"

The woman was delighted at the thought that her daughter was going to marry the king himself. She wasn't worried about the five skeins. "When that comes to it," she said to her daughter later, "we'll find a way out of it. More likely, though, he'll have clean forgotten about it."

So the king and the girl were married. And for eleven months the girl ate as much food as she liked and bought all the dresses she wanted and kept whatever company she wished.

As the days of the eleventh month passed, the girl began to think about those skeins and wondered whether the king was thinking about them too. But the king said not a word, and the girl was quite sure he had forgotten them.

On the very last day of the month, though, the king led her up to a room in the palace she had never set eyes on before. There was nothing in it but a spinning wheel and a stool.

"Now, my dear," says the king, "you'll be shut in here tomorrow with some food and some flax. And if you haven't spun five skeins before dark, your head will be cut off."

Then away went the king to do everything a king has to do.

Well, the girl was that frightened. She had always been such a giddy girl, and she didn't know how to spin. She didn't know what to do next morning, with no one beside her and no one to help her. She sat down on a stool in the palace kitchen and heavens! how she did cry.

All of a sudden, however, she heard a sort of knocking low down on the door. So she stood up and opened it, and what did she see but a small little black thing with a long tail. That looked up at her, all curious, and that said, "What are you crying for?"

"What's that to you?" says the girl.

"Never you mind," that says. "You tell me what you're crying for."

"That won't do me no good if I do," the girl replies.

"You don't know that," that said, and twirled its tail round.

"Well!" she says. "That won't do me no harm if that don't do me no good." So she told him about the pies and the skeins and everything.

"This is what I'll do," says the little black thing. "I'll come to your window every morning and take the flax; and I'll bring it back all spun before dark."

"What will that cost?" she asks.

The thing looked out of the corners of its eyes and said, "Every night I'll give you three guesses at my name. And if you haven't guessed it before the month's up, you shall be mine."

The girl thought she was bound to guess its name before the month was out. "All right!" she says. "I agree to that."

"All right!" that says, and lork! how that twirled that's tail.

Well, next morning, the king led the girl up to the room, and the flax and the day's food were all ready for her.

"Now there's the flax," he says. "And if it isn't spun before dark, off goes your head!" Then he went out and locked the door.

The king had scarcely gone out when there was a knocking at the window.

The girl stood up and opened it and sure enough, there was the little old thing sitting on the window ledge.

"Where's the flax?" it says.

"Here you are!" she says. And she gave it the flax.

When it was early evening, there was a knocking again at the window. The girl stood up and opened it, and there was the little old thing, with five skeins over its arm.

"Here you are!" that says, and it gave the flax to her. "And now," it says, "what's my name?"

"What, is that Bill?" she says.

"No!" it says, "that ain't." And that twirled that's tail.

"Is that Ned?" she says.

"No!" it says, "that ain't." And that twirled that's tail.

"Well, is that Mark?" says she.

"No!" it says, "that ain't." And that twirled that's tail faster, and away it flew.

When the girl's husband came in, the five skeins were ready for him. "I see I shan't have to kill you tonight, my dear," he says. "You'll have your food and your flax in the morning," he says, and away he went to do everything a king has to do.

Well, the flax and the food were made ready for the girl each day, and each day the little black impet used to come in the morning and return in the early evening. And each day and all day the girl sat thinking of names to try out on the impet when it came back in the evening. But she never hit on the right one! As time went on towards the end of the month, the impet looked wickeder and wickeder, and that twirled that's tail faster and faster each time she made a guess.

So they came to the last day of the month but one. The impet returned in the early evening with the five skeins, and it said, "What, hain't you guessed my name yet?"

"Is that Nicodemus?" she says.

"No! 't'ain't," that says.

"Is that Samuel?" she says.

"No! 't'ain't," that says.

"Ah well! Is that Methusalem?" says she.

"No! 't'ain't that either," it says. And then that looks at the girl with eyes like burning coals.

"Woman," that says, "there's only tomorrow evening, and then you'll be mine!" And away it flew!

Well, the girl felt terrible. Soon, though, she heard the king coming along the passage; and when he had walked into the room and seen the five skeins, he says, "Well, my dear! So far as I can see, you'll have your skeins ready tomorrow evening too. I reckon I won't have to kill you, so I'll have my supper in here tonight." Then the king's servants brought up his supper, and another stool for him, and the two of them sat down together.

The king had scarcely eaten a mouthful before he pushed back his stool, and waved his knife and fork, and began to laugh.

"What is it?" asks the girl.

"I'll tell you," says the king. "I was out hunting today, and I got lost and came to a clearing in the forest I'd never seen before. There was an old chalkpit there. And I heard a kind of sort of humming. So I got off my horse and crept up to the edge of the pit and looked down. And do you know what I saw? The funniest little black thing you ever set eyes on! And what did that have but a little spinning wheel! That was spinning and spinning, wonderfully fast, spinning and twirling that's tail. And as it spun, it sang,

"Nimmy nimmy not,
My name's Tom Tit Tot."

Well, when the girl heard this, she felt as if she could have jumped out of her skin for joy; but she didn't say a word.

Next morning, the small little black thing looked wicked as wicked when it came for the flax. And just before it grew dark, she heard it knocking again at the window pane. She opened the window and that

came right in on to the sill. It was grinning from ear to ear, and ooh! that's tail was twirling round so fast.

"What's my name?" that says, as it gave her the skeins.

"Is that Solomon?" she says, pretending to be afraid.

"No! 't'ain't," that says, and it came further into the room.

"Well, is that Zebedee?" she says again.

"No! 't'ain't," says the impet. And then that laughed and twirled that's tail until you could scarcely see it.

"Take time, woman," that says. "Next guess, and you're mine." And that stretched out its black hands towards her.

The girl backed away a step or two. She looked at it, and then she laughed and pointed a finger at it and sang out:

> "Nimmy nimmy not,
> Your name's Tom Tit Tot."

Well! When the impet heard her, that gave an awful shriek and away it flew into the dark. She never saw it again.

BILLY

Billy wasn't born a cripple. He fell out of the apple tree when he
was four and broke both his legs. He broke them in several places.
There was no doctor within a day's ride of the village, so the two
wise women laid poor Billy on a table, and prepared splints, and set his
legs as best they could. The legs set crooked, though, very crooked, and
from that day forward Billy was unable to walk.

While his friends played chase and turned cartwheels, and flexed their
lengthening limbs, all Billy could do was haul himself along on a pair of
blackthorn sticks. Everyone liked him though. They had no end of time
for him because he was cheerful and brave, and made the most of his life.
His friends always carted him round to their games and gatherings.

When he grew up, Billy became a tailor. The little cripple sat cross-
legged in his cottage surrounded by bright rings of talk and laughter. And
after supper, he used to swing along on his sticks in the direction of the
village pub.

One Hallowe'en, while Billy and his friends were sitting in the pub, a band of guisers burst in with howls and shouts. The boys wore girls' clothing, the girls wore shirts and trousers, and all their faces were blackened with soot. At once they blew out the publican's two paraffin lamps, which stood at each end of the bar, and then they swung their own turnip lanterns in front of the drinkers.

Billy and his friends stared at the swinging faces – their fiery eyes and rough-cut mouths, their glow and flicker. And later, when the guisers had been given food and drink and gone on their way, leaving behind them an aftertow of quiet and emptiness, the publican said: "That's scared off the ghosts, then."

A log hissed and spat in the grate.

"There'll be ghosts in the churchyard, though," said a voice.

"That's no place to be tonight," another voice exclaimed.

"I'm not frit!" said Billy quickly.

"The churchyard," said the publican. "That's alive tonight…"

"I'm not frit," said Billy again. "I'll go to the churchyard. I'll sit and sew there all night."

Laughing and alert, Billy's friends carried him back to his cottage to collect cloth and needle and thread; then they took one of the farmer's carts and rolled the cripple up the hill to the graveyard.

"Come on, Billy!" said a voice.

In the moonlight the tailor sat down on a flagstone, and spread out his cloth. It was so bright that he could see to sew. Billy sewed until eleven o'clock, and sewed until twelve o'clock… "See you in the morning, Billy," said several voices.

Then Billy heard a rumble of a voice from the headstone right behind him. The grave began to open and Billy was showered with fistfuls of sand. Out came a head and the head thundered, "Do you see this head without flesh or blood?"

"Yes," said the tailor, "I see that, but I sew this."

"Do you see this arm without flesh or blood?"

"Yes," said the tailor, "I see that, but I sew this."

"Do you see this body without flesh or blood?"

"Yes," said the tailor, "I see that, but I sew this."

By now a huge man, eight foot tall, had come out of the grave. As he started to speak again, Billy finished his piece of sewing; he raised the cloth to his mouth and bit off the thread.

Then the thing reached out and clawed at Billy with its huge bone-hand.

The little tailor leaped up. He pelted across the churchyard and jumped right over the wall.

"Do you see this? Do you see this?" shouted the tailor. And he ran all the way home, laughing.

THREE HEADS OF THE WELL

Less than twelve months after the death of his wife, the king at
Colchester married for a second time. He married for money.
The king's new wife had a nature as bad as her looks (she was
hook-nosed, hump-backed and had yellow skin), and her dowdy daughter
was little better. From the very day they moved into the palace, they
began to spread false rumours about Eleanor, the king's own daughter.

"Too pretty for her own good," the new queen said.

"And knows it," said her daughter.

"Smiles at her father," said the queen.

"And stabs him in the back," her daughter said.

"The king wants my money," said the queen. "And I want you to
inherit the crown. You, not sweet Eleanor!"

So the whisperings went on – suggestions that Eleanor had disobeyed
her father in this way or that, accusations in the king's ear that his own
daughter was tart and even spiteful to her new stepmother and stepsister.

Eleanor was already unhappy at her mother's death; now she suffered more as her father began to harden against her. And the princess felt quite powerless to overcome the growing distance between them. There was no place for Eleanor in her own home.

Early one morning, Eleanor found her father walking in the palace gardens. "I want to go on a journey," she said.

"Maybe," said the king. "Maybe it's for the best."

For some time, neither of them spoke. The bees hummed around them. There were long pale sleeves of cloud overhead.

"I'll go miles and miles," said Eleanor. "I'll see what I see and meet whom I meet."

"I'll give you some money," said the king. "And I'll ask your stepmother to pack some clothes and food for you."

The queen soon had a bundle ready for her stepdaughter: no money, no clothes; nothing but a canvas bag containing coarse bread, cheese and a bottle of beer.

So Eleanor left the court and Colchester and followed a track through a beechwood. Late in the afternoon she entered a glade and there she saw an old man sitting on a stone at the mouth of a cave.

The track led Eleanor right up to the old man. As she approached him, he called out, "Good day, young lady!"

"Good day!" said Eleanor.

"And where are you off to?" he asked. "What's the hurry?"

"I'm going miles and miles," said the princess. "I'll see what I see and meet whom I meet."

"Ah!" said the old man. "What have you got in that bag?"

"Bread and cheese," said Eleanor.

"Brown bread and hard cheese and a bottle of beer. Would you care for some?"

"Thank you, young lady," said the old man, and he gave Eleanor a toothless smile.

When the old man had eaten, he stood up and thanked the princess again for her kindness. "Just beyond this wood," he said, "you'll come to a thick and thorny hedge. There's no way round it and it looks quite impassable. Take this rowan twig," said the old man. "Strike the hedge three times with it, and say, 'Hedge, hedge, let me pass through!'"

"Hedge, hedge, let me pass through!" repeated Eleanor.

"The hedge will open at once," said the old man. "Then a little further on, you'll find a well. Sit down beside it, and almost at once three golden heads will come up out of it."

"And then?" said Eleanor.

"The heads will speak. And you must do whatever they ask of you."

Eleanor promised the old man that she would follow his instructions. When she came to the hedge, she struck it three times, and spoke the right words, and the hedge opened. Then she found the well, and sat down beside it and at once a golden head came up, singing

"Wash me, comb me,
Lay me down softly,
And lay me on a bank to dry,
So that I look pretty
When somebody comes by."

"I will," said Eleanor. She took her silver comb out of her pocket, and combed the head's golden hair. Then she lifted the head out of the dark water and set it down beside the well on a bank thick with wildflowers.

At once the second and third heads came up, and sang the same song. So the princess combed their hair too and laid them beside the first head on the bank of wildflowers. Then she sat down herself and, feeling hungry, opened her canvas bag.

Before long, one of the heads said, "What shall we do for this girl who has been so kind to us?"

"She's beautiful already," said the first head. "But I'll make her quite enchanting."

"I'll make her body and her breath more fragrant than the most sweetly scented flowers," said the second head.

"And my gift will be no less," said the third head. "This girl's a king's daughter. I'll give her a happy marriage to the best of all princes."

After this, the three heads asked Eleanor to let them down into the well again. Then the princess continued her journey. It was already late in the afternoon, and the sun was dipping; small birds sang charms round Eleanor's head.

Now the path led through a splendid park where huge old oaks stood separate and swung at ease. Through the trees, Eleanor could see huntsmen and a pack of hounds and then, as they rode closer, a royal banner.

The princess stepped off the path; she had no wish to talk to kings.

But the king saw Eleanor. He rode up to her and, what with her great beauty and her fragrant breath, he was so bewitched that he escorted her straight back to his castle.

How the king paid court to her! For day after day, he wove fine words and teased her and wooed her. And Eleanor, she was charmed, and she fell in love with the king.

Then the king ordered white cloth and green cloth and cloth of gold for Eleanor; he set aside rooms in the castle for her use, he gave her rings and brooches and necklaces.

So the king and the princess were married. And then, and only then, did Eleanor tell her husband that she was the daughter of the king of Colchester. Her husband laughed. He ordered chariots to be made ready so that they could pay Eleanor's father a visit. And the king's own chariot was padded with purple cloth and inlaid with blood-red garnets and gold disks.

At Colchester the king had been restless and uneasy since his daughter left court. When Eleanor found him, just as she had left him, walking alone in the palace gardens, he was overjoyed to see her and astonished at the splendour of her clothes and jewellery.

Then the princess called for her husband, and the young king told the old king all that had happened.

The court at Colchester trembled with excitement: ladies wondered what to wear, bells rang, fine dishes were prepared, the musicians tuned their fiddles and cleared their throats. Only two people failed to join the dance: the queen and her dingy daughter.

"May she curdle!" sneered the queen.

"Let her hair fall out and her eyes jaundice," sniffed her daughter, "and her teeth turn green."

No sooner had Eleanor left court for her new home, taking a fine dowry with her, than the king's stepdaughter announced that she intended to go on a journey to seek her fortune.

"I'll see what I see and meet whom I meet," said the girl.

Her mother gave her a soft leather bag, stuffed with sweetmeats and sugar cakes and almonds and, at the bottom, a large bottle of the best dry Malaga sherry.

The girl dressed herself in her best travelling clothes, complete with a cloak with a silver clasp and strawberry satin lining. Then she left the court and Colchester and for a long time followed a track through the beechwood.

Late in the afternoon, the girl saw the old man sitting on a stone at the mouth of a cave.

"Good day, young lady!" the old man called out. "Where are you off to? And what's the hurry?"

"What's that to you?" said the girl rudely.

"What have you got in that bag then?" asked the old man.

"Good food and good drink! All sorts of good things," the girl replied. "But they needn't trouble you."

"Won't you give me a mouthful?" the old man asked.

"No," said the girl. "You miserable beggar! Not a drop, unless you promise to choke on it!"

"Bad luck to you!" muttered the old man. "Bad luck go with you!"

The girl turned on her heel and walked on to the thick and thorny hedge. She saw a gap in it but, as she was stepping through it, the hedge closed on her. The thorns pricked her cheeks and arms and legs. By the time she had got through, she was scratched and bleeding.

The girl looked around to see if there was any water – a pool, even a puddle – in which to wash herself. Then she saw the well, and plumped herself down beside it.

At once a golden head came up, singing

> "Wash me, comb me,
> Lay me down softly,
> And lay me on a bank to dry,
> So that I look pretty
> When somebody comes by."

The girl pulled the bottle of Malaga sherry out of the sack and banged the golden head with it. "Take that!" she said. "That's for your washing."

Then the second and third heads came up, and they met with no better treatment than the first.

"What shall we do for this girl?" said one head, bobbing in the dark water, "who has been so cruel to us?"

"I'll give her sores," said the first head, "all over her face."

"Her breath smells bad already," said the second head, "but I'll make it smell far worse."

"She needs a husband and she can have a husband," said the third head. "A poor country cobbler."

The girl walked on. That night she slept under the stars and the next morning she reached a little market town. The people in the market shrank at the sight of the girl's face.

One cobbler, though, felt sorry for the suffering girl. "You poor old creature," he said. "Where have you come from?"

"I," said the girl, "am the stepdaughter," she said, "of the king of Colchester."

The cobbler raised his eyebrows; his leather face creased and wrinkled in a thinking smile.

"Well!" he said. "If I can cure your face and give you good breath, will you reward me by making me your husband?"

"I will," said the girl. "With all my heart I will."

"This box of ointment," said the cobbler, "is for your sores, and this bottle of spirits is for your breath." (Not long before he had mended the shoes of a penniless old hermit who had given him the box and the bottle as payment.)

"Every day," said the cobbler, "smear the ointment over your sores, and take a nip of these spirits."

The girl did just as the cobbler told her. Within a few weeks, she was not only cured but somewhat more presentable than before. She and the cobbler got married and, after a day or two, set out on foot for the court of Colchester.

When the queen discovered that her daughter had married a poor cobbler, she was so upset that she hanged herself. So the king at Colchester inherited her vast wealth, as he had always hoped to do.

"And out of this fortune," said the king to the cobbler, "I'll give you the sum of a hundred pounds provided you take my stepdaughter away – take her away to the furthest corner of my kingdom and stay there with her."

So this is what the cobbler did. He lived in a little village for many years, mending shoes, and his wife brought in a little extra money by weaving. She made cloth and dyed it all the colours of the rainbow and sold it at market.

HUGHBO

The only house on the little island was low-slung and whitewashed. In stormy weather it was swept by sea-fret, and in every season scolded by wind; and that was where Peter lived on his own.

For as long as it was light, he worked the land. He ploughed and sowed and reaped as his father and mother had done before their drowning; he made hay, he milked his cows and cut the peats. And each Sunday morning, he rowed over to the mainland to visit his sweetheart.

In the evenings, Peter lit candles in his kitchen and sat yawning beside the fire. Through the door, in the stable, he could hear the lowing of his cows and the snuffling of his pigs as they settled down for the night.

One night, when the wind was going wild outside, the young farmer climbed into his box-bed and was just about to blow out the candle when he saw the dark corner beside the stable door was gleaming. Peter looked more carefully, and made out the figure of a little crouching man. He was naked from head to toe, and his leathery brown skin shone in the dark.

"Lord!" said the farmer, and he gripped the sides of his bed, not for one moment taking his eyes off the ugly creature – his squashed nose and puffy lips and large ears, the flat bald crown of his head, his stringy seaweed hair and beard.

Then Peter jumped out of bed. With one hand he grabbed his psalmbook, and with the other he picked up his cut-throat.

"Hughbo! I'm Hughbo!" jabbered the creature.

The farmer crossed himself with the psalmbook, and made a circle in the air with his cut-throat.

The ugly creature didn't move. He didn't step forward into the kitchen or back through the door into the stable. He just watched the young man and repeated, "I'm Hughbo!"

Then Peter picked up the iron poker and tongs and threw them at the creature. But the little man ducked the first and side-stepped the second.

Peter was afraid and angry. He unhooked the metal pot hanging from its chain above the fire and with both hands started to swing it…

At this the little man darted forward. He grabbed the rim of the pot.

"Get out!" shouted Peter, swinging both fists and catching the creature one blow on his ribs and another on the back of his head.

But the little man was as light on his feet as a cat. He leaped across the kitchen and, with a yell, disappeared through the stable door.

Peter rubbed his eyes, and wondered what to do. And within a minute, the ugly creature crept back into the corner of the kitchen and started grinning at him.

"I'm Hughbo!" said the creature, and he pointed to himself.

"What do you want?" said Peter.

"I live in the briny."

"What do you want here?"

"Sick and tired of gnawing dead men's bones," said the creature.

"Do you want bread?" asked Peter.

The creature grinned. "I'll work for my lodging."

"I said nothing about lodging," Peter replied, looking at the creature's leathery skin and seaweed hair.

But the ugly little man went on grinning. "Hughbo work well! Every night I'll grind the quern."

Peter narrowed his eyes. Busy that he was, he wasn't sorry at the offer of help. *I'll judge him by his work*, he thought, *not by his looks!*

And so the young farmer agreed that Hughbo would grind the quern each night and make enough meal for the farmer's morning plate of porridge. In return, Peter allowed Hughbo to sleep on the threshold between the kitchen and the stable, and to take one saucer of milk each morning to add to his own supply of parched barley.

That same night, Peter lay in bed and watched the gleaming creature turning the quern in the corner of the kitchen; he closed his eyes and fell asleep to the wind's skirl and the gritty chuckle of the quernstones.

In the morning, the farmer was well pleased with his clean, sharply ground meal. And after only a few days, he began to feel quite at home with his strange sea-visitor, and to welcome his company.

Each Sunday, when he rowed over to the mainland to see her, Peter told Janey more about Hughbo – his friendliness and readiness to work and dependability.

"I don't know how I'd manage without him," said the young man. And twice he rowed Janey out to the island so that she could see Hughbo for herself.

"All leather and kelp and not a stitch of clothing," Janey exclaimed. "And that gleam! I'll never get used to him."

"I have," said Peter.

One summer day the young farmer married Janey and brought her back to his little wind-loud island. How happy they were! At first light they rose and, after cooking the meal Hughbo had ground for them, they worked in the fields together; in the afternoon, Janey stayed in the farm, and cleaned and sewed and cooked; and when Peter came in at dusk, they ate supper and talked and laughed; they sat close to each other in front of the fire; they went to bed early.

Hughbo always took care not to disturb Peter and Janey, and ate his food in the stable, and when Janey saw him standing alone and naked at the quern, she began to feel sorry for him.

"The nights are getting chill," she said to herself. "If my man cares for Hughbo, I must care for him too."

On her next visit to the mainland, Janey bought some cloth. During the next week she cut out and sewed a fine cloak for Hughbo with a hood to cover his bald head. "That should please him," she said to herself, "and please my man too."

When it was finished, Janey spread the cloak over the quernstones, just before getting into bed.

"What are you doing?" asked the young man.

"Coming to bed!" said Janey.

As usual, Hughbo entered the kitchen quietly so as not to disturb the young man and his wife. But as soon as he saw the new cloak hanging over the quernstones, Hughbo began to moan and to sob.

Peter and Janey sat up in the dark.

"Hughbo!" said Peter. "Hughbo! What's wrong?"

Round and round the quern the little man stumped, sobbing and saying again and again:

> "Hughbo's got a cloak and hood,
> So Hughbo can do no more good
> Hughbo's got a cloak and hood,
> So Hughbo can do no more good."

Then, without even looking in the direction of the young man and his wife, Hughbo threw open the farmhouse door and plunged out into the wind and the darkness. And search for him as they did, Peter and Janey, they never saw Hughbo again.

MONDAY, TUESDAY

Poor Lusmore! He was all misshapen. His legs were bowed, and the hump on his back was as big as a football. When he stood up, he seemed almost to be squatting; and when he sat down, he rested his chin on his knees for support.

Lusmore's arms, though, were strong and tanned, and his fingers were nimble. Almost every day he sat on his low stool outside the cottage where he lived with his old parents – he was almost thirty himself – and plaited rushes and straw into baskets and hats. And he always got a good price for his work because everyone felt so sorry for him.

Everyone talked about him too, of course! Out of his hearing, people said all kinds of things about Lusmore. They said no human being could be as deformed as he was, and that he must be a changeling. They said he warbled strange words to himself. They said he was a master of magic and medicine.

Lusmore seemed unaware of all this. His daily suffering had made him gentle and sweet. He was glad he was alive. He loved birds and butterflies. Every morning in summer, he tucked a foxglove through the band of his straw hat, and sang as he worked, and eagerly greeted each and every passer-by.

One day, Lusmore rode on the back of a cart into the town of Caher, and sold his baskets and hats in the market there. He did a brisk trade, and went off to drink a few beers afterwards. But when he returned to the deserted market-place, it was late, the light was failing, and the cart and its driver were nowhere to be seen. Poor Lusmore! He had no choice but to walk home.

The little hunchback trudged out of Caher down the road towards Cappagh, and by the time he reached the old moat at Knockgrafton it was already quite dark. Lusmore hauled his sad shape of a body off the road and over the molehills and tussocks and sat down on the edge of the old grassy ditch.

"And I'm not halfway home," said Lusmore, and he gave a great sigh – the kind he only permitted himself when no one else was nearby.

The hunchback sat cross-legged, his chin resting on one knee, and looked at the gibbous moon. Lumpen clouds were swarming over it, and it seemed as if the moon were running, or rolling as fast as she could without getting anywhere.

"Like me!" said Lusmore, and he smiled ruefully. "Just like me! I'm a poor moon-calf."

Lusmore pressed his chin against his knee and closed his eyes. He listened to the shushing of the light wind in the old lime trees down the road; and then he heard rising above the wind and out of the grassy moat a different sound, clearer and higher in pitch – a song without words. It was the sound of many voices, sweet voices, so mingling and blending that they sounded like one voice. Then the voices began to sing words: "Monday, Tuesday, Monday, Tuesday, Monday, Tuesday…" At this, they paused for a moment, and then they began the melody again.

Lusmore was spellbound by the singing. *Though to be sure,* he thought to himself, *there's not much variety to it.* After a while, the hunchback began to hum the melody in tune with the voices; and then, when they paused, he sang out "Wednesday".

"Monday, Tuesday…" sang the voices and Lusmore sang with them. "Monday, Tuesday, Monday, Tuesday…" And then, for a second time, "Wednesday".

When the little people heard Lusmore, they were delighted. They skipped and eddied up the bank, and swirled him down to the bottom of the moat in a whirlwind of cries and laughter. The hunchback was twirled round and round, light as a piece of straw, and the fairy fiddlers played faster and faster.

When the world stopped spinning, Lusmore saw he had been swept into a fine fairy pavilion. True, it was rather low ceilinged, but that didn't bother him! The whole place was lit with candles and packed out with little people – little people chattering, eating, playing fiddles and pipes and harps, dancing…

Lusmore was made most welcome: he was given a low stool, and provided with food and drink.

"Grand! I feel grand!" he said as one fairy after another enquired whether he had all he needed, and praised his skill as a singer. "Just grand!" said Lusmore. "I might as well be the king of the whole land!"

Then the music faltered and stopped; the dancers stood still; the feasters put down their knives and forks. Lusmore watched as the little people crowded together in the middle of the pavilion, and began to whisper. Now the hunchback began to feel nervous: "For all your kindness and courtesy," he muttered, "you fairy folk, you're fickle and chancy."

As Lusmore watched, one little man left the huddle and walked up to him. He smiled at Lusmore and solemnly he said:

"Lusmore! Lusmore!
That hump you wore,
That hump you bore
On your back is no more;
Look down on the floor!
There's your hump, Lusmore!"

As the hunchback looked down, his ugly hump fell from his shoulders and dropped to the ground. Little Lusmore felt so light; he felt so happy; like the cow in the story of the cat and the fiddle, he could have jumped over the moon.

But seeing the hump was scarcely enough! Lusmore raised his arms and clasped the back of his neck. Then very slowly, for fear of bumping his head against the ceiling, Lusmore lifted his head. For the first time in his life, he stood upright.

Lusmore laughed and then he cried. The fair pavilion, the little people crowding around him, they were all so beautiful. Lusmore began to feel dizzy; his eyesight became dim; he slipped gently to the ground, and fell fast asleep.

When Lusmore woke, the sun was already well up. The dewy grass… cows chewing the cud… the moat at Knockgrafton… Then he remembered! He crossed himself. And still lying on the grass, he reached out with one hand and felt behind his back.

When Lusmore was sure that the hump was not there, he leaped up. He got down on his knees and said his prayers. Then he saw he was wearing a new suit of clothes, and shook his head, grinning.

So Lusmore stepped out for Cappagh, feeling as light as a piece of thistledown. He had such a spring in his step that you might have thought he had been a dancing-master all his life. His mother and father and all the people living in the village were astonished at the sight of him – indeed at first glance many of them did not even recognise him. And it wasn't long before the story of how Lusmore had lost his hump was taken to Caher, and then spread for miles and miles around; it was soon the talk of everyone in the midlands of Ireland.

Lusmore had learned to live with his misfortune and now he took his good fortune with a shrug and a smile. Free of his ugly load, he delighted in his dapper appearance, but he had no wish to harum-scarum off to Dublin or climb Croagh Patrick or drink himself into an early grave. He was already in the place he loved, and he was among the friends and neighbours he had known since the day of his birth. He went on with his old job of plaiting rushes and straw.

One morning, Lusmore was sitting in the sunlight outside his cottage door when a woman walked up to him.

"This is the road to Cappagh?" she asked.

"This is Cappagh," Lusmore replied. "Who are you looking for?"

"I've come from County Waterford," said the woman. "Over thirty miles. I'm looking for one Lusmore."

"I know him," said Lusmore.

"He had the hump taken off him by the fairies," said the woman. "Is that right?"

"It is," said Lusmore, smiling.

"Well, the son of a neighbour of mine – Jack – Jack Madden the cobbler – he's got a devil of a hump on him. That'll soon be the death of him…"

"I am Lusmore," said the little man.

"You!" exclaimed the woman. "Well! There's an omen!"

Lusmore was quite happy to tell the woman what had happened at the old moat at Knockgrafton. He explained about the tune the fairies had sung, and how he had joined in and added to it, and about the fair pavilion, the whispering fairies…

The woman thanked Lusmore. She hurried back down the long lanes to her own country. She went straight to her neighbour and it wasn't more than a couple of days before the two of them arranged for a horse and cart to take them and Jack Madden all the way back to Knockgrafton.

On the way there, Jack's mouth was full of complaints. "This jolting," he said. "That'll be the death of me! It's all right for you!" He complained his mother would make him work twice as hard to pay for the cost of the cart. He complained at the taste of the ale they had brought with them. What with his peevishness and the noise of the cart, Jack's mother and her neighbour were worn out by the time they reached the moat at Knockgrafton.

"Don't forget what we've told you," they said. "We'll be back at sunrise." Then the cart rolled away down the road to Caher and Jack Madden was left on his own in the darkness under the rising moon.

Jack hauled his sad shape of a body off the road and over the molehills and tussocks and sat down on the edge of the old grassy ditch. The stillness of the place wrapped itself round him: the clucking of a bird, settling down for the night; a far barking; acres of silence.

And then, out of this silence, from somewhere down in the moat, rose sweet singing, high-pitched clear singing that made Jack Madden catch his breath and listen intently. The fairies were singing their song just as Lusmore had shaped it for them.

"Monday, Tuesday," they sang, "Monday, Tuesday, Monday, Tuesday, Wednesday." There was no pause in their singing now; the melody and words were continuous.

Jack Madden's spirit was as shapeless as his body. He had no grace about him, and little sense of the fitting. He listened to the little people sing their song seven times and then, without regard for timing and without thought for pitch, he stood up and bawled out, "WEDNESDAY, THURSDAY."

If one day is good, thought Jack, *two days are better. I should get two suits of clothing*!

The fairies whirled up the grassy bank. They lifted Jack off his feet and swept him down to the bottom of the moat and into their pavilion. There they jostled around him, picking at his clothing and banging him with their tiny fists, screeching and screaming, "Who spoiled our tune? Who spoiled our tune?"

Then one little man raised his hand and the crowd of angry fairies fell back. The little man narrowed his eyes at Jack and said:

> "Jack Madden! Jack Madden!
> Your words were all wrong
> For our sweet lovely song.
> You're caught in our throng
> And your life we will sadden:
> Here's two lumps for Jack Madden."

At this, a troop of twenty of the strongest fairies staggered into the pavilion, carrying Lusmore's hump. They walked over to poor Jack and at once slammed it down on his back, right over his own hump. And as soon as they had done so, it became firmly fixed there, as if it had been nailed down with six-inch nails by the best of carpenters. Then the little people screeched and screamed again, and kicked Jack out of their pavilion into the dark night.

In the morning, Jack Madden's mother and her neighbour came back from Caher. They found Jack lying just outside the moat, with a double hump on his back; he was half-dead.

The two women looked at him; they looked at each other; but for fear of the fairies, they said nothing. They lifted poor Jack and laid him moaning in the bottom of the cart, and rode straight home to Waterford.

What with the terrible weight of his second hump, and the strain of the long jolting journey, Jack Madden didn't live long. "My curse," he muttered just before he died, "my curse on any fool who listens to a fairy tune!"

SAMUEL'S GHOST

Poor little Samuel! He was asleep when his cottage caught fire, and when he woke up it was too late. He was only a lad and he was burned to death; he got turned into ashes, and maybe cinders.

After a while, though, Samuel got up. The inside of him got up and gave itself a shake. He must have felt rather queer: he wasn't used to doing without a body, and he didn't know what to do next, and all around him there were boggarts and bogles and chancy things, and he was a bit scared.

Before long, Samuel heard a voice. "You must go to the graveyard," said whatever it was, "and tell the Big Worm you're dead."

"Must I?" said Samuel.

"And ask him to have you eaten up," said the something. "Otherwise you'll never rest in the earth."

"I'm willing," said Samuel.

So Samuel set off for the graveyard, asking the way, and rubbing shoulders with all the horrid things that glowered around him.

By and by, Samuel came to an empty dark space. Glimmering lights were crossing and recrossing it. It smelt earthy, as strong as the soil in spring, and here and there it gave off a ghastly stink, sickening and scary.

Underfoot were creeping things, and all round were crawling, fluttering things, and the air was hot and tacky.

On the far side of this space was a horrid great worm, coiled up on a flat stone, and its slimy head was nodding and swinging from side to side, as if it were sniffing out its dinner.

Samuel was afraid when he heard something call out his name, and the worm shot its horrid head right into his face. "Samuel! Is that you, Samuel? So you're dead and buried, and food for the worms, are you?"

"I am," said Samuel.

"Well!" said the worm. "Where's your body?"

"Please, your worship," said Samuel – he didn't want to anger the worm, naturally – "I'm all here!"

"No," said the worm. "How do you think we can eat you? You must fetch your corpse if you want to rest in the earth."

"But where is it?" said Samuel, scratching his head. "My corpse?"

"Where is it buried?" said the worm.

"It isn't buried," said Samuel. "That's just it. It's ashes. I got burned up."

"Ha!" said the worm. "That's bad. That's very bad. You'll not taste too good."

Samuel didn't know what to say.

"Don't fret," said the worm. "Go and fetch the ashes. Bring them here and we'll do all we can."

So Samuel went back to his burned-out cottage. He looked and looked.

He scooped up all the ashes he could find into a sack, and took them off to the great worm.

Samuel opened the sack, and the worm crawled down off the flat stone. It sniffed the ashes and turned them over and over.

"Samuel," said the worm after a while. "Something's missing. You're not all here, Samuel. Where's the rest of you? You'll have to find the rest."

"I've brought all I could find," said Samuel.

"No," the worm said. "There's an arm missing."

"Ah!" said Samuel. "That's right! I lost an arm I had."

"Lost?" asked the worm.

"It was cut off," said Samuel.

"You must find it, Samuel."

Samuel frowned. "I don't know where the doctor put it," he said. "I can go and see."

So Samuel hurried off again. He hunted high and low, and after a while he found his arm.

Samuel went straight back to the worm. "Here's the arm," he said.

The worm slid off its flat stone and turned the arm over.

"No, Samuel," said the worm. "There's something still missing. Did you lose anything else?"

"Let's see," said Samuel. "Let's see… I lost a nail once, and that never grew again."

"That's it, I reckon!" said the worm. "You've got to find it, Samuel!"

"I don't think I'll ever find that, master," said Samuel. "Not one nail. I'll give it a try, though."

So Samuel hurried off for the third time. But a nail is just as hard to find as it's easy to lose. Although Samuel searched and searched, he couldn't find anything; so at last he went back to the worm.

"I've searched and searched and I've found nothing," said Samuel. "You must take me without my nail – it's no great loss, is it? Can't you make do without it?"

"No," said the worm. "I can't. And if you can't find it – are you quite certain you can't, Samuel?"

"Certain, worse luck!"

"Then you must walk! You must walk by day and walk by night. I'm very sorry for you, Samuel, but you'll have plenty of company!"

Then all the creeping things and crawling things swarmed round Samuel and turned him out. And unless he has found it, Samuel has been walking and hunting for his nail from that day to this.

THE CHANGELING

Last week there was a wonder.
Up at Hawes's there was a birth, a son to follow four bonny daughters. Such a scowl of a night, but no one was paying any attention to that. There was singing and dancing, all the neighbours in.

They swaddled him in a mesh of muslin,
They swathed him in pure rainbow silk…

That was the Tuesday, and they arranged with me to baptise the bairn on the Sabbath.

But Saturday morning there was a horrible yelling coming out of the cradle. And when Mrs Hawes looked in, she saw her bairn had turned yellow and ugly. His nose was a sort of snout, his milkskin had become leathery, and his teeth were already coming through.

Mrs Hawes cried out, and the farmer and his neighbours, they all rubbed their eyes. It made no difference, of course. The little bairn just lay there and squinted up at them and threshed its legs, and yelled.

Poor Mrs Hawes, she's a fragile woman and she was in a terrible state. When she tried to feed the bairn, he tore at her poor breasts. He wrestled around, and groused and grizzled and, one way and another, the farmer and his family were unable to get a minute's sleep for the next three nights.

That was when they sent for my lass Janey, and asked her to try her hand. She knows what's what, Janey, just like her mother. She won't stand any nonsense.

Out trooped the farmer and his family, and off to the market. They were all heartily glad to see the back of the little bairn, and to get the sound of that yammering out of their ears.

Janey promised Mrs Hawes she would be patient. After all… the poor wee bairn, it was so ugly and so sad, and seemed so unhappy with this bright world.

But what with all the weeping and wailing, Janey finally lost her temper. She yelled right back at the bairn, and told him that his mewling was stopping her from winnowing the corn and grinding the meal.

The bairn looked up then and opened its eyes as wide as can be. "Well, Janey," it said, clear as clear, with a knowing look. "Well, Janey, loose the cradle-band! Watch out for your neighbours and I'll work your work."

Then that wee devil climbed out of his cradle. He stretched and grinned and strolled out of the house. He cut the corn, he fed the livestock in the fields; then the wind got up and the mill began to turn…

Janey's knees were knocking together. She wasn't going to show it, though. She knew that would only turn bad into worse. So when the wee devil had finished the work and strolled back into the house again, she fed him and played with him until the farmer and his family came home.

As soon as she saw them out of the window, Janey popped the bairn back into the cradle. And at that, the caterwauling began all over again.

Then Janey took Mrs Hawes down to the kitchen and told her straight out what had happened. Poor Mrs Hawes! "What shall I do, Janey? Help me, Janey!"

"The wee devil!" said Janey. "Leave him to me! I'll cook some trouble for him."

At midnight, Janey asked Hawes if he would climb up on to the farmhouse roof and lay three bricks across part of the top of the chimney pot, and she told his wife to work the bellows until the fire was glowing – a bed of red hot coals.

Then my lass, she stripped that wee scrap, she undressed him and threw him on to the burning coals.

The little wee fellow shrieked and he screamed.

At once there was a rustling sound, quickly growing, like wind before rain. And then a rattling at the windows and tapping, tapping at the chimney and banging at the farmhouse doors. That was the fairies, right enough.

"In the name of God," shouted Janey, "bring back the bairn!"

Darkness and wind! The casement window screeched. They brought back the bairn then; they laid him safely in his mother's lap.

And the wee devil? He flew up the chimney laughing.

MOSSYCOAT

There was once a poor old widow who lived in a little cottage. She had one daughter who was nineteen and very beautiful. Day after day her mother busied herself spinning a coat for her.

A pedlar came courting this girl. He called at the cottage regularly, and kept bringing her this trinket and that trinket. He was in love with her, and badly wanted her to marry him.

But the girl wasn't in love with him; things didn't work out as easily as that. She didn't know quite what to do for the best, and asked her mother for advice.

"Let him come," said her mother. "Get what you can out of him while I finish this coat. After that, you won't need him or his pretty little presents. You tell him, girl," the mother said, "that you won't marry him unless he gets you a white satin dress embroidered with sprigs of gold as big as a man's hand; and mind you tell him it must be a perfect fit."

Next time the pedlar came round, and asked the daughter to marry him, she told him just this – the very same words her mother had used.

The pedlar looked at the girl, and took stock of her size and build. And within a week, he was back with the dress. It was made of white satin and embroidered with sprigs of gold, and when the girl went upstairs with her mother and tried it on, it was a perfect fit.

"What shall I do now, mother?" asked the girl.

"Tell him," said her mother, "that you won't marry him unless he gets you a dress made of silk the colour of all the birds of the air. And it must be a perfect fit."

The girl told the pedlar this, and in two or three days he was back at the cottage with the coloured silk dress. And since he knew her size from the first dress, of course it was a perfect fit.

"Now what shall I do?" asked the girl.

"Tell him," said her mother, "that you won't marry him unless he gets you a pair of silver slippers that are a perfect fit."

The girl told the pedlar just this, and in a few days he called round with them. The girl's feet were only about three inches long, but the slippers were a perfect fit. They were not too tight; neither were they too loose.

Once more the girl asked her mother what she should do.

"I can finish the coat tonight," said her mother, "and then you won't need the pedlar. Tell him," she said, "that you'll marry him tomorrow. Tell him to be here at ten o'clock."

The girl told the pedlar just this. "Ten o'clock in the morning," she said. "I'll be there, my love," said the pedlar. "By heaven, I will!"

That night the girl's mother worked on the coat until very late, but she finished it all right. Green moss and gold thread, that's what it was made of: just those two things. "Mossycoat", the woman called it; and that's what she called the daughter she had made it for.

"It's a magic coat," she said. "A wishing coat! When you've got it on, you have only to wish to be somewhere, and you'll be there that very instant. And you've only to wish if you want to change yourself into something else, like a swan, or a bee."

Next morning the widow was up at dawn. She called her daughter, and told her that it was time for her to go out into the world and seek her fortune. "And a handsome fortune it must be," she said.

"What about the pedlar?" asked the girl.

"I'll send him packing when he comes round," said her mother. "Don't give him another thought."

The old widow was a seer and knew what was going to happen. She gave her daughter the mossycoat and a gold crown. "Take the two dresses and silver slippers as well," she said. "But travel in your working clothes."

So Mossycoat was ready to set off, and she put on her coat of green moss and gold thread.

"Wish yourself a hundred miles away," her mother said. "Then keep walking until you come to a big hall, and ask for a job there. You won't have far to walk, my blessed. They're bound to find you work at the big hall."

Mossycoat did as her mother told her, and soon she found herself in front of a big house belonging to a gentleman. She knocked at the front door and said she was looking for work. Well, the long and the short of it was that the mistress of the house herself came down to see her; and her ladyship liked the look of her.

"What work can you do?" she asked.

"I can cook, your ladyship," said Mossycoat. "In fact, people say I'm a very good cook."

"I can't employ you as cook," the lady said. "I've got one already. But I'll engage you to help the cook, if that will satisfy you."

"Thank you, your ladyship," said Mossycoat. "I'll be really happy in this house."

So it was settled that Mossycoat was to be the undercook. And after her ladyship had showed her up to her bedroom, she took her down to the kitchen and introduced her to the other servants.

"This is Mossycoat," she told them, "and I've engaged her," she said, "to be the undercook."

Then the mistress of the house left them, and Mossycoat went up to her bedroom again, to unpack her belongings, and hide away her gold crown and silver slippers, and her silk and satin dresses.

The other kitchen girls were beside themselves with jealousy; and it didn't help matters that the new girl was far more beautiful than any of them.

"Here's this vagrant in rags," one girl said, "and she's put above us."

"All she's fit for," said another, "is work in the scullery."

"Undercook!" cried a third girl. "If anyone's going to be undercook, it should be one of us."

"One of us," said the fourth girl. "Not a girl in rags and tatters picked up off the street."

"We'll put her in her place!" the girls said. "That we will!"

So they went on and on until Mossycoat came down again, ready to start work. Then they really set about her.

"Who on earth do you think you are, setting yourself above us?"

"You're going to be the undercook, are you?"

"No fear!"

"What you're going to do is scour the pans."

"And polish the knives."

"And clean the grates."

"And that's all you're good for."

Then down came the milk-skimmer on the top of her head, pop, pop, pop.

"That's what you deserve," they told her. "And, my lady, that's what you'll get."

So that is how things were for Mossycoat. She was given all the dirtiest work, and soon she was up to her ears in grease, and her face was as black as soot. And every now and again one or another of the servants would pop, pop, pop her on top of the head with the skimmer, until Mossycoat's head was so sore she could scarcely stand it.

Days turned into weeks, weeks into months and Mossycoat was still scouring the pans and polishing the knives and cleaning the grate; and the servants were still pop, pop, popping her on the head with the skimmer.

Now there was going to be a big dance in a grand house nearby. It was to last three nights, with hunting and other sports during the daytime. All the gentry from miles around were going to be there; and of course the master and mistress and their son – they only had one child – planned to be there.

This dance was all the talk among the servants.

"I wish I could go," said one girl.

"I'd like to dance with some of those young gentlemen," said a second.

"I'd like to see what dresses the ladies wear," said a third.

And so they all went on – all except Mossycoat.

"If only we'd the clothes," said one, "we'd be all right. We're just as good as their ladyships any day."

"And you, Mossycoat," said another. "Wouldn't you like to go?"

"You'd look just right in all your rags and dirt," they said.

And down came the skimmer on Mossycoat's head, pop, pop, pop. Then they all laughed at her. What crude people they were!

Now Mossycoat was very handsome, and no amount of rags and dirt could hide the fact. The other servants might think as they liked, but the young master had his eye on Mossycoat, and the master and mistress had always taken particular notice of her, because of her fine looks.

On the first day of the big dance, they sent for her and asked her if she would like to come with them.

"Thank you," said Mossycoat, "but I'd never dream of such a thing. I know my place better than that. Besides," she said, "I'd cover one side of the coach with grease. And I'd sully the clothes of anyone I danced with."

The master and mistress made light of that, but no matter what they said, they were unable to change Mossycoat's mind.

When Mossycoat got back to the kitchen, she told the other servants why she had been sent for.

"What! You?" exclaimed one servant. "I don't believe it!"

"If it had been one of us, that would have been different."

"You'd grease all the gentlemen's clothes – if there are any who would dance with a scullery girl."

"And the ladies, they'd be forced to hold their noses when they walked past you."

"No," they said, "we don't believe the master and mistress ever asked you to go to the ball with them. You must be lying," they said.

And down came the skimmer on top of her head, pop, pop, pop.

On the next evening, the master and the mistress, and their son too, asked Mossycoat to go to the dance.

"It was a grand affair last night," said the master.

"And it'll be even grander this evening," added the mistress.

"Do come with us," said their son. "Mossycoat, I beg you."

But Mossycoat said no. She said she couldn't go on account of her rags and her grease and her dirt. Even the young master was unable to persuade her, and it wasn't for want of trying.

The other servants refused to believe Mossycoat when she told them that she had been invited again to the dance, and added that the young master had been very pressing.

"Listen to her!" they cried. "What next? What an upstart! And all lies!" they said.

Then one of the servants snorted and grabbed the skimmer and down it came once again, pop, pop, pop, on Mossycoat's head.

That night, Mossycoat decided to go to the dance, all dressed up, and all on her own, without anybody knowing about it.

The first thing she did was to put all the other servants under a spell. As she moved around, she just touched each of them, without being noticed, and each fell asleep as soon as she did so.

Next, Mossycoat had a really good wash, her first since she had come to the big house. She had never been allowed to before. The other servants had made her dirty and kept her dirty.

Then Mossycoat went up to her bedroom. She threw off her working clothes and shoes, and put on her white satin dress embroidered with gold sprigs, her silver slippers, and her gold crown. And, of course, underneath the dress, she was wearing the mossycoat.

When she was ready, Mossycoat just wished herself at the dance; and as soon as she had spoken, there she was! She did just feel herself soaring up and flying through the air, but only for a moment. Then she was standing in the ballroom.

The young master noticed Mossycoat standing on her own, and once he had seen her, he was unable to take his eyes off her. He had never seen anyone so handsome, nor so beautifully dressed, in his life.

"Who is she?" the young man asked his mother.

"I don't know," said the mistress. "I've never seen her before."

"Can't you find out, mother?" he said. "Can't you go and talk to her?"

The young man's mother saw he would never rest until she did, so she walked up and introduced herself to the young lady, and asked her who she was, and where she came from, and so on. But all she could get out of her was that she came from a place where they hit her on the head with a skimmer.

After a while, the young master went over and introduced himself, but Mossycoat didn't tell him her name; she gave nothing away.

"Well, will you dance with me?" asked the young master.

"Thank you," said Mossycoat, "but I'd rather not."

But the young man stayed at Mossycoat's side. He kept asking her to dance, over and over again.

"All right!" said Mossycoat. "Just once."

The young man and Mossycoat danced once, up the length of the ballroom and back down again; and then Mossycoat said she had to leave. The young man pressed her to stay, but it was a waste of breath; she was determined to go, there and then.

"All right," said the young man. "I'll come and see you off."

But Mossycoat just wished she were back in the big house, and there she was! So the young master wasn't able to see her off! She vanished from his side in the twinkling of an eye, leaving him there gaping in astonishment.

Thinking she might be out in the entrance hall, or in the porch, waiting for her carriage, the young man went out to look for her; but there was no sign of her anywhere, inside or out, and no one he asked had seen her leave. The young man went back to the ballroom, but he was unable to think of anything or anyone but the mysterious girl, and took no further interest in the ball.

When Mossycoat got back to the big house, she made sure that all the other servants were still under her spell. Then she went up to her bedroom and changed into her working clothes; and when she had done that, she came down to the kitchen again and touched each of the servants.

That broke the spell and woke them. One by one they started up, wondering what time of day it was, and how long they had been asleep.

"A long time!" said Mossycoat. "The whole evening, in fact! The mistress wouldn't like to know about this, would she?"

The servants begged Mossycoat not to let on, and offered her bribes to keep quiet about it. They gave her a skirt, a pair of shoes, a pair of stockings, some stays; they were all old enough but they still had a bit of wear in them. So Mossycoat promised to say nothing about it.

And that night, they didn't hit her over the head with the skimmer.

All next day the young master was restless. He could think of nothing but the young lady he had seen the night before and fallen in love with at first sight. He kept wondering whether she would be at the dance again that evening, and how he could stop her from disappearing.

I must find out where she lives, he thought. *Otherwise, how will I be able to bear it when the dance is over?*

"I'll die," the young man told his mother, "if I'm not able to marry her." He was madly in love with her!

"Well," said his mother, "she seemed a nice, modest girl. But she wouldn't say who she was or who her family are. She wouldn't say where she came from, except that it was a place where they hit her on the head with a skimmer!"

"She's a mystery, I know," said the young man, "but that doesn't mean I want her any the less. I must marry her, mother," he said, "whoever she is and whatever she is. That's God's truth, mother, and strike me dead if it isn't!"

It wasn't long before the young master and this wonderful, handsome lady he had fallen in love with were all the talk in the kitchen.

"And fancy you, Mossycoat, thinking he especially wanted you to go to the dance," they said. And then they really set about her, making all kinds of sarcastic remarks, and hitting her on the head with the skimmer, pop, pop, pop, for lying to them.

It was just the same later on, too, when Mossycoat returned to the kitchen after declining to go to the dance for the third time. "This is your last chance," said the servants. "You're such a liar, Mossycoat! We'll give you one more chance." And down came the skimmer on the top of her head, pop, pop, pop.

Then Mossycoat put the whole devil's breed of them under a spell just as she had done the night before, and got herself ready to go to the dance. The only difference was that this time she put on her other dress – the dress made of silk the colour of all the birds of the air. And underneath the dress, she was wearing the mossycoat, of course.

When Mossycoat entered the ballroom, the young master was watching and waiting for her. His horse was ready saddled and standing at the door. He went over to the young lady and asked her for a dance.

She said just the same as on the night before: no at first, and in the end, yes. And as soon as they had danced up the length of the ballroom and back down again, she said she had to leave. This time, however, the young man kept his arm round the girl's waist until they got outside.

But then Mossycoat wished she were back in the big house, and almost as soon as she had spoken, she was there! They young man felt her rise into the air but he was unable to do anything about it. Maybe he did just touch her foot, though, because she dropped one slipper.

The young man picked up the slipper. But as for catching up with the girl, it would have been easier to catch up with the wind on a stormy night.

As soon as she got home, Mossycoat changed back into her old clothes. Then she released the servants from the spell. When they realised that they had fallen asleep again, one offered her a shilling and another half-a-crown – a third of a week's wages – not to let on; and once again Mossycoat promised to keep quiet about it.

The young master spent the next day in bed, dying for the love of the young lady who had dropped one of her silver slippers on the previous night. The doctors were unable to do anything for him at all, so the young man's parents decided to make his condition known. They said the only person able to save his life was the young lady whose foot fitted the silver slipper – and that the slipper was only about three inches long. They promised that if she would come forward, the young master would marry her.

Ladies came from near and far, some with big feet and some with small, but none small enough for the silver slipper, however much they pinched and squeezed. Poor women came too, but it was just the same for them. And of course, all the servants tried on the slipper, but that was out of the question altogether.

All this time, the young master lay dying.

"Is there no one else?" asked his mother. "No one else at all? No rich lady? No poor woman?"

"No one," they said. "No one at all. Everyone has tried it on except for Mossycoat."

"Tell her to come here at once," said the mistress.

So the other servants fetched Mossycoat.

"Mossycoat!" said the mistress. "Try this slipper on."

Mossycoat slipped her foot into it easily enough; it was a perfect fit. Then the young master jumped out of bed and opened his arms…

"Wait!" said Mossycoat, and she ran out of the room. Before long, though, she was back again wearing her satin dress with gold sprigs, her gold crown and both her silver slippers. Again the young master opened his arms…

"Wait!" said Mossycoat, and again she ran out of the room. This time she came back wearing her silk dress the colour of all the birds of the air. Mossycoat didn't stop the young master this time, and he took her into his arms and kissed her.

After all this, when at last the master and the mistress and the young man and Mossycoat had time to talk to one another quietly, there were one or two questions they wanted to ask her.

"How did you get to the dance and back again in no time?" they said.

"Just wishing," said Mossycoat. And she told them about the magic coat her mother had made for her, and the powers it gave her when she cared to use them.

"That explains everything!" said the mistress.

"But what did you mean," asked the master, "when you said you came from a place where they hit you on the head with a skimmer?"

"I mean just what I said," replied Mossycoat. "The skimmer's always coming down on my head, pop, pop, pop!"

The master and mistress were furious when they heard that. All the kitchen servants were told to leave and the dogs were sent after them to drive them right away from the place.

Then Mossycoat sent for her old mother and the master and mistress made her welcome at the big house. Mossycoat and the young master got married on the first day possible, and Mossycoat had a coach-and-six to ride in; she could have had a coach-and-ten if she had wanted, for as you can imagine her every wish was granted. The young man and Mossycoat were always happy together. Mossycoat's mother lived with them, and they had a basketful of children.

KING OF THE CATS

I suppose I can think myself lucky. There's plenty in our village who are drawing unemployment, and I know two more – three if you count Dan, he's taking early retirement – who reckon they'll be laid off before Christmas. At least people need me; and they always will.

It's not all laughs, mind. The only ones who thank you are the early birds. And then you're all on your own, and you're out in every weather, too. And the old flowers, the pulpy heaps of them, they smell sickly sweet!

You get some weird experiences, I can tell you. Weird and wonderful!

One evening last summer I was out late; the vicar said they needed it for nine in the morning. I was having my break, sitting on the edge like, and swinging my legs. Well, I took a nip or two and I was so tired that I reckon I fell asleep.

A cat woke me up. "Miaou!" And when I opened my old eyes, it was almost dark and I was down at the bottom.

I stood up and peered over the edge and you know what I saw? Nine black cats! They all had white chests and they were coming down the path, carrying a coffin covered with black velvet. My! Oh my! I kept very quiet but I still had a careful look. There was a little gold crown sitting on top of the black velvet. And at every third step the cats all paused, solemn like, and cried "Miaou!"

Then the cats turned off the path and headed straight towards me. Their eyes were shining, luminous and green. Eight of them were carrying the coffin and a big one walked in front of them, showing them the way. One step, two steps, three steps: miaou!

When they got to the graveside, they stopped. They all looked straight at me. My! Oh my! I felt queer.

Then the big cat, the one at the front, stepped towards me. "Tell Dildrum," he said in a squeaky voice, "tell Dildrum," he said, "that Doldrum is dead."

Then he turned his back on me and led away the other cats with the coffin. One step, two steps, three steps: miaou!

As soon as they were out of the way, I scrambled out of the grave, and I was glad to get home, I can tell you. There they all were: my Mary cross-eyed with knitting and Mustard hopping around his cage and old Sam stretched out in the corner. Everything as usual; the clock ticking on the mantelpiece.

So I told the old girl about the talking cat and the coffin and the crown. She gave me one of those looks – a sort of gleam behind her specs.

"Yes, Harry," she said.

"It's true, Mary," I said. "I couldn't have made it up. And who is Dildrum anyhow?"

"How should I know?" said Mary. "That's enough of your stories. You're upsetting old Sam."

Old Sam got up. First he prowled around and then he looked straight at me. My! Oh my! I felt very queer again.

"That's just what the cat said," I said. "Not a word more and not a word less. He said, 'Tell Dildrum that Doldrum is dead.' But how can I?

How can I tell Dildrum that Doldrum is dead if I don't know who Dildrum is?"

"Stop, Harry!" shouted Mary. "Look at old Sam! Look!"

Old Sam was sort of swelling. Swelling and staring right through me. And at last he shrieked out, "Doldrum – old Doldrum dead? Then I'm the King of the Cats!"

He leaped into the fireplace and up the chimney, and he has never been seen again.

DATHERA DAD

The kitchen was a magic box, full of light and dancing shadows. Shafts of winter sunlight lanced the range and the dresser and the pail of milk, and the hawthorn tree shivered outside the window.

The kettle sang, and the farmer's wife hummed as she put the large saucepan of water on the range, then mixed the ingredients – flour and eggs and breadcrumbs, sugar, salt, suet, then nutmeg and cinnamon and spice.

"And now the brandy," she said, pouring a generous dollop into the mixture, and then a second dollop for good measure.

The farmer's wife put the mixture into a white bowl and covered it with muslin tied round the rim. Then she lowered it into the steaming water.

As soon as the pudding felt the heat of the water, it jumped out of the saucepan. It rolled over the sunlit range and fell on to the floor, cracking the white bowl. It wheeled across the floor towards the farmer's wife.

At that moment there was a loud knock and Tom the tramp put his head round the back door.

"Morning, missus," he said. "Can you spare a pair of shoes?"

"I can't, Tom," said the farmer's wife.

"Christmas, missus."

"Here! You can have this pudding, then," said the farmer's wife, bending down and picking up the pudding in the cracked white bowl. "Christmas pudding!"

Tom was only a few yards down the frosty road when he felt something rolling around in the sack slung over his back. He stopped and opened the sack.

Then the pudding rolled on to the road. The white bowl broke into pieces, and the pudding burst open… And out stepped a little fairy child who took one look at Tom the tramp and cried, "Take me home to my dathera dad! Take me home to my dathera dad!"

SEA-WOMAN

It was an empty, oyster-and-pearl afternoon. The water lipped at the sand and sorted the shingle and lapped round the rock where the girl was sitting.

Then she saw a seal, like a mass of seaweed almost, until she gazed into those eyes. It swam in quite close, just twenty or thirty water-steps away.

She looked at the seal; the seal looked at her. Then it barked. It cried out in a loud voice.

She stood up on her rock. She called out to the seal: not a word but a sound, the music words are made of.

The seal swam in a little closer. It looked at the girl. Then it cried. Oh! The moon's edge and a mother's ache were in that cry.

The girl jumped off the rock. Her eyes were sea-eyes, wide and flint-grey. "Seal!" she cried. "Sea-woman! What do you want?"

And what did the seal want but the girl's company? As she padded down the strand, it followed her, always keeping fifteen or twenty water-steps away, out in the dark swell. The girl turned back towards her rock, and the seal turned with her. Sometimes it huffed and puffed, sometimes it cried, it wailed as if it were lost, all at sea.

The girl bent down and picked up a curious shell, opaline and milky and intricate.

"Listen, listen!" sang the wind in the shell's mouth.

Then the girl raised the shell and pressed it to her right ear.

"One afternoon," sang the shell, "oyster-and-pearl, a man came back from the fishing. He was so weary. He peeled off his salt-stiff clothing. He washed. For an hour or two hours he closed his eyes. And then, when the moon rose, he came strolling along this strand.

"He listened to the little waves kissing in the rocks. He smelt earth on the breeze and knew it would soon rain. This is where he walked, rocking slightly from side to side, in no hurry at all for there was nowhere to go.

"Then he stopped. Down the beach, no more than the distance of a shout, he saw a group of sea-people dancing. They were singing and swaying; they danced like the waves of the sea.

"Then the sea-people saw him. At once they stopped singing and broke their bright ring. As the fisherman began to run towards them, they turned towards a pile of sealskins – in the moonlight they looked like a wet rock – and picked them up and pulled them on and plunged into the water.

"One young woman was not so quick, though. She was so caught up in the dance that the fisherman reached her skin before she did. He snatched it up and tucked it under one arm. Then he turned to face the sea-woman, and he was grinning.

" 'Please,' she said. Her voice was high as a handbell and flecked with silver. 'Please.'

"The fisherman shook his head.

" 'My skin,' said the sea-woman. There she stood, dressed in moonlight, reaching out towards him with her white arms; and he stood between her and the sea.

" 'I've landed some catches,' breathed the fisherman, 'but never anything like this …'

"Then the young woman began to sob. 'I cannot,' she cried. 'I cannot go back without my skin.'

"*… and this catch I'll keep,* thought the fisherman.

" 'My home and my family and my friends,' said the sea-woman.

"Now she wept and the moon picked up her salt tears and turned them into pearls. How lovely she was, and lovely in more ways than one: a young woman lithe as young women are, a sea-child, a sister of the moon. For all her tears, the fisherman had not the least intention of giving her back her skin.

" 'You'll come with me,' he said.

"The sea-woman shuddered.

"Then the man stepped forward and took her by the wrist. 'Home with me,' he said.

"The sea-woman neither moved towards the man nor pulled away from him. 'Please,' she said, her voice sweet and ringing. 'The sea is my home, the shouting waves, the green light and the darkening.'

"But the fisherman had set his heart against it. He led the sea-woman along the strand and into the silent village and back to his home.

"Then the fisherman shut the door on the sea-woman and went out into the night again to hide the skin. He ran up to the haystack in the field behind his house, and loosened one of the haybricks and hid the skin behind it. Within ten minutes, he was back on his own doorstep.

"The sea-woman was still there; without her skin, there was nowhere for her to go. She looked at the man. With her flint-grey eyes she looked at him."

For a moment the girl lowered the shell from her ear. She gazed at the emptiness around her, no one on the beach or on the hillslope leading down to it, no one between her and the north pole. The little waves were at their kissing and the seal still kept her company, bobbing up and down in the welling water.

"Listen, listen!" sang the wind in the shell's mouth.

The girl raised the shell again and pressed it to her right ear.

"Time passed," sang the shell, "and the sea-woman stayed with the fisherman. Without her skin, she was unable to go back to the sea, and the fisherman was no worse than the next man.

"For his part, the fisherman fell in love. He had spent half his life on the ocean. He knew all her moods and movements and colours, and he saw them in the sea-woman.

"Before long the man and the woman married, and they had one daughter and then two sons. The sea-woman loved them dearly and was a good mother to them. They were no different from other children except in one way:

there was a thin, half-transparent web between their fingers and their toes.

"Often the woman came walking along the strand, where the fisherman had caught her. She sat on a rock; she sang sad songs about a happier time; and at times a large seal came swimming in towards her, calling out to her. But what could she do? She talked to the seal in the language they shared; she stayed here for hours; but always, in the end, she turned away and slowly walked back to the village.

"Late one summer afternoon, the sea-woman's three children were larking around on the haystack behind their house. One of the little boys gave his sister a push from behind, and the girl grabbed wildly at the wall of the haystack.

"One haybrick came away. And the skin, the sealskin that the fisherman had hidden in one stack after another as the years passed, fell to the ground.

"The children stopped playing. They fingered the skin; they buried their faces in its softness; they took it back to show their mother.

"The sea-woman dared scarcely look at it and looked at it; dared scarcely touch it and touched it.

" 'Mother!' said the children, crowding around her. 'What is it?'

"The sea-woman pulled her children to her. She dragged them to her and squeezed them. She hugged and kissed each of them. Then she turned and ran out of the house with her skin.

"The children were afraid. They followed her. They saw her pull on the skin, cry a great cry, and dive off a rock. Then a large seal rose to meet her and the two seals leaped and dipped through the water.

"When their father came back from the fishing, his children were standing at the stone jetty.

" 'You go home,' said the man. 'I'll come back in an hour.'

"Slowly the man waded in his salt-stiff clothing along this strand. He kept rubbing his pale blue eyes and looking out across the dancing water.

"She rose out of the waves. She was no more than a few water-steps away.

" 'Husband!' she cried. 'Husband! Look after our children! Take care of our children!' Her voice carried over the water. 'You've loved me and looked after me, and I've loved you. But for as long as I lived with you, I always loved my first husband better.'

"Then the sea-woman, the seal-woman, slipped under the sallow waves once more. One moment she was there; the next, she was not there…"

The girl took the opaline shell away from her ear, and set it down on the sand. For a long time she sat there. The seal had gone; it had deserted her and the dark water shivered.

CHARGER

"I 'll just have to sell old Charger," said the farmer.

"Not Charger!" exclaimed his wife.

"He's one too many," the farmer said. "The other two are yearlings now."

So the farmer set off for the autumn Horse Fair. He rode Charger up the rainswept dale, feeling rather glum at the prospect of losing his loyal horse, and none too pleased at the thought of having to walk ten miles to get home again from the Fair.

In the high hills, the farmer met a pedlar, a small little man with a wrinkled face, dressed from top to toe in chestnut brown. He was struggling through the wind and rain, carrying a battered old suitcase.

"Would you sell your horse?" said the little man.

"That's just what I'm going to do," the farmer replied.

"How much?" asked the little man.

The farmer narrowed his eyes. "You could have him for eight pounds," he said.

"No!" said the little man. "Not eight! I'll give you seven." And he dropped a hand into his pocket.

Well now, thought the farmer, *which is better: seven pounds for Charger here and now, or eight at the Fair – or seven, or six?* The farmer looked at the poor wet little man. He thought of the long walk home. "It's a deal," he said.

So the farmer dismounted and the man counted the coins into his hand: "One, two, three, four, five, six, seven."

"That's it," said the farmer.

Then the little man picked up his battered suitcase. He raised one foot as high as his hip, wedged it into a stirrup and swung up into the saddle.

And there and then, right in front of the round-eyed farmer, the little man and Charger sank into the earth.

THE THREE BLOWS

The stone farmhouse seemed to grow out of the grey-green skirt of the mountain. The walls were lichenous, one part of the roof was covered with slate and the other part with turf. The whole building was so low slung it seemed to be crouching.

It wasn't alone. Megan could stand at their door (you had to stoop to get in or out) and see three other smallholdings within reach, almost within shouting distance. And no more than a mile away, along the track north and west, huddled and patient, was the little village of Llanddeusant.

But when the wind opened its throat and rain swept across the slopes; when the lean seasons came to Black Mountain; when wolves circled the pens and small birds left their sanskrit in the snow: the farm seemed alone then, alone in the world – and all the more so to Megan since her husband had died leaving her to bring up their baby son and run the farm on her own.

But Megan was a hard-working woman. As the years passed, her holding of cattle and sheep and goats so increased that they strayed far and wide over Black Mountain. And all the while her son grew and grew until he became a big-boned young man: rather awkward, very strong-willed, and shy and affectionate. Yet sometimes, when she looked at him sitting by the fire, lost in his own sliding dreams, it seemed to Megan that she didn't really quite know her son. *He's like his father*, she thought. *Something hidden. What is he thinking?*

Gwyn spent most of his time up on Black Mountain, herding the cattle and sheep and goats. More often than not he followed them up to a remote place in a fold of the mountain: it was a secret eye, a dark pupil that watched the sun and moon and stars: the little lake of Llyn y Fan Fach.

One spring morning, Gwyn was poking along the edge of the lake, on his way to the flat rock where he sometimes sat and spread out his provisions – barley-bread, maybe, and a chump of cheese, a wooden bottle seething with ale. Gwyn clambered on to the rock and stared out across the lake, silver and obsidian. And there, sitting on the glassy surface of the water, combing her hair, he saw a young woman. She was using the water as a mirror, charming her hair into ringlets, arranging them so that they covered her shoulders; and only when she had finished did she look up and see Gwyn, awkward on the rock, open-mouthed, arms stretched out, offering her bread…

Slowly, so slowly she scarcely seemed to move at all, the young woman glided over the surface of the water towards Gwyn and, entranced, he stepped down to meet her.

And then Gwyn heard her voice. It was like a bell heard long ago and remembered: very sweet and very low. "Your bread's baked and hard," she said. "It's not easy to catch me."

Which is just what Gwyn tried to do. He lunged into the lake, and at once the girl sank from sight; she left her smile behind, playing on the smooth surface of the water.

For a while Gwyn stood and stared. A stray cloud passed in front of the sun; the water shivered. Gwyn felt as if he had found the one thing in this world that mattered only to lose it. And he resolved to come back, to find the girl and catch her, whatever the cost.

Gwyn turned away from the lake. He set off down the string-thin sheep-runs, the network that covered the steep shoulders of the mountain. At first he walked slowly, but by the time he reached the doors of his farmhouse he was almost running, so eager was he to tell his mother about the bewitching girl he had seen up at Llyn y Fan Fach.

"Stuff!" said Megan. "You and your dreams." But as she listened to Gwyn, she did not doubt that he was telling the truth. Perhaps she saw in the young man at her hearth another young man at the same hearth long before, shining and stammering. But then she quailed as she thought of what might become of Gwyn if he was caught up with the fairy folk.

"I won't be put off," said Gwyn. "I won't be put off if that's what you're thinking."

"Leave her alone, Gwyn," said Megan. "Take a girl from the valley."

"I won't be put off," said Gwyn.

"You won't catch her," Megan said, "not unless you listen to me."

"What do you mean?" said Gwyn.

" 'Your bread's baked and hard.' Isn't that what she said?"

Gwyn nodded.

"Well, then. Take up some toes. Take up some toes. Stands to reason."

"Toes?" said Gwyn.

"Pieces of dough. Unbaked and just as they are."

Gwyn followed his mother's advice. As night began to lose its thickness, yet before you could say it was dawn, he filled one pocket with dough, and quietly let himself out of the farmhouse without waking his mother. He sniffed the cool air and began to climb the dun and misty mountain.

She was not there. Shape-changing mist that plays tricks with the eyes dipped and rose and dipped over the dark water until the sun came down from the peaks and burned it away. Birds arrived in boating parties, little fish made circles, and she was not there.

Not long before dusk, Gwyn saw that two of his cows were lumbering straight towards the top of the dangerous escarpment on the far side of the lake. He stood up at once and began to run round the lake after them. "Stupids!" he bawled. "You'll lose your footing."

Then she was there. She was there, sitting on the shimmer of the water, smiling, just as she had done on the day before.

Gwyn stopped. He reached out his arms and, as the beautiful young woman drifted towards him, he gazed at her: the blue-black sheen of her hair, her long fingers, the green watersilk of her dress, and her little ankles and sandals tied with thongs. Then Gwyn dug into his pockets and offered her the unbaked dough and not only that but his hand too and his heart for ever.

"Your bread is unbaked," said the young woman. "I will not have you." Then she raised her arms and sank under the surface of the water.

Gwyn cried out, and the rockface heard and answered him, all hollow and disembodied. But even as he looked at the lake and listened to the sounds, each as mournful as the other, Gwyn thought of the girl's smile and was half-comforted.

"I'll catch you," he said.

"You caught the cows," said Megan later that evening. "That's what matters."

Gwyn grinned.

"Anyhow," said Megan, "you're not going up there again, are you?"

"You know I am," said Gwyn.

"In that case," said his mother, "listen to me. I'd take some partly baked bread up with you."

Gwyn reached Llyn y Fan Fach again as day dawned. He kept a watch on the lake and his whole face glowed – his cheeks and chin and ears and eyes, above all his eyes – as if he had just turned away from a leaping fire. He felt strong and he felt weak.

This time it was the sheep and goats that strayed towards the rockface and scree at the far end of the lake. But Gwyn knew how nimble-footed they were. Even when they loosened and dislodged a rock that bumped and bundled down the escarpment and splashed into the lake, they were in no danger.

All morning wayward April shook sheets of sunlight and rain over the lake and then, in the afternoon, the clouds piling in from the west closed over the mountain. For hour after hour, Gwyn crouched on the smooth rock or padded round the rim of the lake. Now he was no longer so excited or fearful; the long waiting had dulled him.

In the early evening, the mood of the weather changed again. First Gwyn could see blue sky behind the gauze of cloud, and then the clouds left the mountain altogether. The lake and the ashen scree were soothed by yellow sunlight.

This was the hour when Gwyn saw that three cows were walking on the water. They were out in the middle of Llyn y Fan Fach and ambling towards him.

Gwyn stood up. He swung off the rock platform and down to the lakeside. And as he did so, the young woman appeared for the third time, as beautiful as before, passing over the mirror of water just behind the three cows.

Gwyn stepped into the lake, up to his shins, his thighs, his hips. Still the young woman came on, and she was smiling – an expression that lit up her whole face, and above all her violet eyes.

Gwyn reached out his hands and, wordless, offered her the partly baked bread.

The young woman took the bread, and Gwyn grasped her cool hand. He was nervous and breathless.

"Come with me," he said. "Come to the farm… I'll show you. Come with me… marry me!"

The young woman looked at Gwyn.

"I'll not let you go," said Gwyn. He could hear his voice rising, as if someone else were speaking. "I've waited!" He tightened his grip on the girl's hand.

"Gwyn," said the young woman. "I will marry you," she said, "on one condition."

"Anything!" said Gwyn. "Anything you ask."

"I will marry you and live with you. But if you strike me…"

"Strike you!" cried Gwyn.

"… Strike me three blows without reason, I'll return to this lake and you'll never see me again."

"Never!" swore Gwyn. "Never!" He loosened his fierce grip and at once she slid away, raised her arms, and disappeared under the surface of the water.

"Come back!" shouted Gwyn. "Come back!"

"Gon-ba!" said the mountain. "Gon-ba!"

Gwyn stood up to his waist in the chill water. The huge, red sun alighted on the western horizon and began to slip out of sight.

But now two young women, each as lovely as the other, rose out of the water and a tall old white-headed man immediately after them. At once they came walking towards Gwyn.

"Greetings, Gwyn!" called the old man. "You mean to marry one of my daughters, you've asked her to marry you." He waved towards the two girls at his side. "And I agree to this. You can marry her if you can tell me which one you mean to marry."

Gwyn looked from one girl to the other: their clefs of black hair, their strange violet eyes, their long necks…

One of the girls tossed her charcoal hair; the other eased one foot forward, one inch, two inches, and into Gwyn's memory. The sandals… the thongs…

Gwyn reached out at once across the water and took her cool hand. "This is she," he said.

"You have made your choice?" asked the old man.

"I have," said Gwyn.

"You've chosen well," the man said. "And you can marry her. Be kind to her, and faithful."

"I will," said Gwyn, "and I will."

"This is her dowry," said the man. "She can have as many sheep and cattle and goats and horses as she can count without drawing breath."

No sooner had her father spoken than his daughter began to count for the sheep. She counted in fives, "One, two, three, four, five – one, two, three, four, five" over and over again until she'd run out of breath.

"Thirty-two times," said the man. "One hundred and sixty sheep." As soon as they had been named, the sheep appeared on the surface of the darkening water, and ran across it to the bare mountain.

"Now the cattle," said the old man. Then his daughter began to count again, her voice soft and rippling. And so they went on until there were more than six hundred head of sheep and cattle and goats and horses milling around on the lakeside.

"Go now," said the white-headed man gently. "And remember, Gwyn, if you strike her three blows without reason, she'll return to me, and bring all her livestock back to this lake."

It was almost dark. The old man and his other daughter went down into the lake. Gwyn took his bride's hand and, followed by her livestock, led her down from the mountain.

So Gwyn and the girl from Llan y Fan Fach were married. Gwyn left the house in which he had been born, and his mother in it, and went to a farm a few miles away, outside the village of Myddfai.

Gwyn and his wife were happy and, because of the generosity of the old man, they were rich. They had three sons, dark-haired, dark-eyed, lovely to look at.

Some years after Gwyn and his wife had moved to Myddfai, they were invited to a christening back in Llanddeusant. Gwyn was eager to go but, when the time came for them to set off, his wife was not.

"I don't know these people," she said.

"It's Gareth," said Gwyn. "I've known him all my life. And this is his first child."

"It's too far to walk," said his wife.

"Fetch a horse from the field then," said Gwyn. "You can ride down."

"Will you go and find my gloves," said Gwyn's wife, "while I get the horse? I left them in the house."

When Gwyn came out of the farmhouse with the gloves, eager to be off, his wife had made no move towards the paddock and the horse.

"What's wrong?" cried Gwyn, and he slapped his wife's shoulder with one of her gloves.

Gwyn's wife turned to face him. Her eyes darkened. "Gwyn!" she said.

"Gwyn! Remember the condition on which I married you."

"I remember," said Gwyn.

"That you would never strike me without reason."

Gwyn nodded.

"Be careful! Be more careful from now on!"

Not long after this, Gwyn and his wife went to a fine wedding. The guests at the breakfast came not only from Llanddeusant and Myddfai but many of the surrounding farms and villages. The barn in which the reception was held was filled with the hum of contentment and the sweet sound of the triple harp.

As soon as she had kissed the bride, Gwyn's wife began to weep and then to sob. The guests around her stopped talking. A few tried to comfort her but many backed away, superstitious of tears at a wedding.

Gwyn didn't know quite what to do. "What's wrong?" he whispered. "What's wrong?" But his wife sobbed as bitterly as a little child. Gwyn smiled apologetically and shook his head; then he pursed his lips and dropped a hand on to his wife's arm. "What's the matter?" he insisted. "You must stop!"

Gwyn's wife gazed at her husband with her flooded violet eyes. "These two people," she said, "are on the threshold of such trouble. I see it all. And Gwyn," she said, "I see your troubles are about to begin. You've struck me without reason for the second time."

Gwyn's wife loved her husband no less than he loved her and neither had the least desire that their marriage should suddenly come to an end. Knowing that her own behaviour could surprise and upset Gwyn, she sometimes reminded her husband to be very careful not to strike her for a third time. "Otherwise," she said, "I must return to Llyn y Fan Fach. I have no choice in the matter."

But the years passed. The three boys became young men, all of them intelligent. And when he thought about it at all, Gwyn believed that he had learned his lesson on the way to the christening and at the wedding, and that he and his water-wife would live together happily for as long as they lived.

One day, Gwyn and his wife went to a funeral. Everyone round about had come to pay their last respects to the dead woman: she had been the daughter of a rich farmer and wife to the priest, generous with her time and money, and still in the prime of her life.

After the funeral, a good number of the priest's friends went back to his house to eat funeral cakes with him and keep him company, and Gwyn and his wife were among them.

No sooner had they stepped inside the priest's house than Gwyn's wife began to laugh. Amongst the mourners with their black suits and sober faces, she giggled as if she were tipsy with ale or romping with young children.

Gwyn was shocked. "Shush!" he said. "Think where you are! Stop this laughing!" he said. And firmly he laid a restraining hand on his wife's forearm.

"I'm laughing," said Gwyn's wife, "because when a person dies, she passes out of this world of trouble. Ah! Gwyn," she cried, "you've struck me for the third time and the last time. Our marriage is at an end."

Gwyn's wife left the funeral feast alone and went straight back to their fine farm outside Myddfai. There she began to call in all her livestock.

"Brindled cow, come! White speckled cow, spotted cow, bold freckled cow, come! Old white-faced cow, Grey Squinter, white bull from the court of the king, come and come home!"

Gwyn's wife knew each of her livestock by name. And she did not forget the calf her husband had slaughtered only the previous week. "Little black calf," she cried, "come down from the hook! Come home!"

The black calf leaped into life; it danced around the courtyard.

Then Gwyn's wife saw four of her oxen ploughing a nearby field. "Grey oxen!" she cried. "Four oxen of the field, you too must come home!"

When they heard her, the oxen turned from their task and, for all the whistles of the ploughboy, dragged the plough right across the newly turned furrows.

Gwyn's wife looked about her. She paused. Then she turned her back on the farmhouse and the farm. Those who saw her never forgot that sight: one woman, sad and steadfast, walking up on to Myddfai mountain, and behind her, plodding and trudging and tripping and highstepping, a great concourse of creatures.

The woman crossed over on to the swept slopes of Black Mountain just above the lonely farm where Gwyn had been born and where Megan still lived in her old age. Up she climbed, on and up to the dark eye.

The Lady of Llyn y Fan Fach walked over the surface of the water and disappeared into the water, and all her hundreds of animals followed her. They left behind them sorrow, they left a wake of silence, and the deep furrow made by the oxen as they dragged their plough up over the shoulder of the mountain and into the lake.

THE MULE

Before the three princes were ten, their mother died. That was bad enough and sad enough; ice and snow started to thaw, houses wept and trees wept, the whole country wept on the day she was laid in the grave.

But before they were twenty, the princes lost their father too. He went out over the sea, visiting the king of Cornwall, and on the way back, a mulish storm carried off his boat. The king's body was never found – not even one poor bone; and nothing, not even a bleached rib, was found of his boat.

The three young men walked around the draughty palace; they wandered through the shining gardens, and into the stables. And there, perched on a lintel, was a beautiful bird. She was gold and she was turquoise, and she sang so sweetly that she sang their aches away.

"Let's catch her," said One.

"And cage her," said Two.

They lunged towards the little bird, and the little bird stopped singing and hopped up on to the roof.

"Leave her to me," said Fool.

"You?" exclaimed One and Two.

"Me!" said Fool.

Early next morning Fool climbed up into the stable loft and wedged himself into the window recess: head and shoulders against one wall, feet against the other. Then he opened the little window and waited.

The gold-and-turquoise bird settled once more on the lintel; and One and Two came wandering into the stables and listened to the bird and lunged at her.

When the little bird hopped out of their reach up on to the stable roof, Fool stuck his hand out of the little window and grabbed at her. A throb of turquoise! A fever of gold! The young prince was left with one tail feather in his hand.

Fool looked at the fair feather. And high above his head the bird sang, "Follow me! Follow! Find me! Find me!"

"I will!" said Fool. He scrambled down the loft ladder, ran past his two brothers and out of the stable courtyard. But as fast as he ran, the gold-and-turquoise bird was always just a stone's throw in front of him.

Fool was running so hard that when he came to the flint wall girdling the palace grounds he simply kicked his legs in the air and jumped clean over it.

The young prince landed right on the back of a mule who was having a midday doze in the field on the other side.

"Whoa!" the mule said. "Where are you going?"

"After that bird," said Fool. "See her? I'm following her until I find her."

"Are you a good rider?" asked the mule.

"Middling good," said Fool.

"Hold on so," said the mule. "We'll follow that bird."

"Hurry!" said Fool. "She's gone already."

"I'll take you to the place where that bird lives," said the mule.

On the other side of the mule's field, there was another wall – a double wall. The mule galloped at it, and kicked his legs in the air, and leaped right over it.

"You're the best rider ever I saw," said the mule.

"You're the best mule ever I saw," said Fool.

All day Fool and the mule rode on. They rode through sun and showers and green and silver. The day's brightness faded; the air became cool and misty.

"I'm hungry now," said the mule. "Can you go and get me a few grains of oats?"

"Where from?" said Fool. "I can't see any oats."

"Wait a bit!" said the mule.

But although Fool waited and waited, there was not a brick of building to be seen.

"I'm hungry too," said Fool. "Can you order me a stew? Carrots, knuckles of meat, mushrooms, potatoes, mmm!"

"At the bottom of this hill," said the mule, "there's a stream. Over the stream there's a bridge. And by the bridge, there's an inn. We can eat there!"

"Right," said Fool. "What shall we do for money?"

"Just order my oats as I told you," said the mule.

"How much do you want?" asked Fool.

"Seven stone," the mule said.

"Seven stone!" exclaimed Fool.

"That'll do me," said the mule.

So they stopped at the inn. And when Fool had put the mule into the stable, he went and found the innkeeper and got the mule seven stone of oats.

"Go in now and order your own supper," said the mule.

So Fool went back into the inn and sat down beside the fire. He ate his fill of stew and drank two pints of dark beer and dreamed about the gold-and-turquoise bird.

"So?" said the innkeeper.

"Very tasty!" said Fool.

"Half a guinea," said the innkeeper. "Half of that for the oats and half for the stew."

"I have no money," said Fool. "I should have told you first."

"All right," said the man. "I'll keep that mule in the stable until you can pay me."

"But we're following the bird," said Fool.

"Get out!" shouted the innkeeper.

Then the innkeeper hurried out to lock the stable door. "You're staying with me, old friend," he said to the mule, "until your rascal of an owner…"

The mule took one look at the innkeeper and gave him the devil of a kick in the shins. The man fell over sideways. "You'll pay for this," he cried.

"I'll pay," said the mule. "Later!" The mule stepped over the innkeeper and out of the stable. "Come on now," he said to Fool. "There's a time for everything."

So Fool swung up on to the mule's back and they galloped away into the darkness.

When it began to grow light, and shapes became definite, Fool realised they were riding through country he had never seen before. Everything looked as if it had been made for giants or by giants. All around, there were huge mountains, huge pine trees, huge stone walls…

Before long, Fool and the mule came up to a wall even more gigantic than the others. It was a great stone curtain stretching across the land to left and to right.

"It's five miles high," said the mule.

"It's the end of the world," said Fool.

"Hold on so," said the mule. He broke into a trot, then a gallop, kicked up his legs and leaped right over the mighty wall.

"You're a rider that can't be beaten," said the mule.

"You're a mule that can't be beaten," said Fool.

But another obstacle stood in their way: a huge grey lake, lipping and lapping at their ankles.

"That's five miles long and five miles across," said the mule. "And a good thing too! I'm still feeling thirsty after all those oats."

"Leave it alone," said Fool.

"I'll stop here and have a drink," said the mule.

"You'll weigh yourself down," said Fool. "You won't want to go on."

"You watch and see," said the mule. So Fool dismounted and the mule ambled up to the edge of the lake and began to drink.

The sun was climbing into the sky and, while he was waiting for the mule to slake his thirst, Fool must have shut his eyes; because, when he next took a look in the mule's direction, he saw that he had almost licked the whole lake dry.

"Haven't you had enough?" cried Fool.

"That's better," said the mule. "On we go!"

So Fool mounted the mule once more, and they picked their way across the stony lake basin and up into the neck of a valley.

At the end of the valley, there stood a mountain, and from top to bottom it was on fire – a flickering yellow pyramid. The flames sang in the sunlight. And between this mountain and the two travellers reared a wall built of flagstones, fifteen foot high.

The mule took a look at it. "Hold on now," he said.

"At it, mule!" said Fool.

So the mule flicked his tail and kicked his legs in the air and leaped over the wall.

At once the mule opened his mouth and let out all the lake water he had swallowed, a great drench, a tide that put out every flame on the mountain.

Then from somewhere within the swirl of smoke issued the sound of singing, a song so sweet that it sang their aches away. Out of the smoke flashed the gold-and-turquoise bird. "Follow me! Follow! Find me! Find me!"

Then the little bird winged over the scree into a cave and out of sight.

"Quick, mule!" said Fool.

So the two travellers hurried over the stony mountainside to the entrance of the cave. Into the cave they went. It sloped down and sloped up and then it opened into a great chamber, a lofty room lit by wavering candles, hung with flashing tapestries.

There was no bird there. But there was the most beautiful girl, a princess, dressed in gold-and-turquoise. As soon as Fool saw her, he wanted to live with her for the rest of his life.

"Princess," he said, "will you marry me?"

"I will not," said the princess. "Not unless you can find my father. And that," she said, "I doubt you'll ever do. I've hidden him!"

"Let me stable my mule first," said Fool. "We've come a long way."

"You've a long way to go," said the princess.

So Fool took the mule through the chamber into a stone stable, comfortable enough.

"Now what am I going to do?" said Fool.

"That young lady," said the mule, nodding his old head, "has a broody hen. You'll find it in her bedroom, right under her bed. Under the hen, there are eleven eggs, and one of them is yellow and spotted."

"I'm listening," said Fool.

"The king is inside it. Pick it up and raise your arm, as if you were going to smash it against the flagstone, and the king-in-the-egg will call out, and beg you to spare his life."

"You're the mule!" said Fool. He went straight up to the princess's bedroom, and everything happened just as the mule had predicted.

Fool spared the king's life and then he asked the princess, "Will you marry me now?"

"I will not," said the princess. "Not unless you can find my father again. And that," she said, "you'll never do. I've hidden him for a second time."

When Fool went back to the stable, the mule told him the king was hidden inside the bill of the duck swimming on the big pond in the palace garden.

"What am I to do?" said Fool. "I can't walk on water."

"Have a look at my tail," said the mule. "There's one grey hair in it."

"I have it," said Fool.

"Pull it out!" said the mule. "Take it down to the pond! Float it on the water!"

"What for?" asked Fool.

"The duck will swim straight towards it. Catch hold of the duck, and threaten to slit its throat, and then the king-in-the-bill will call out, and beg you to spare his life."

"You're the mule!" said Fool. He went straight down to the duckpond, and everything happened just as the mule had predicted.

Fool spared the king's life and then he asked the princess, "Now will you marry me?"

"I will not," said the princess. "Not unless you can find my father for a third time."

"The princess has hidden him in a block of wood," said the mule.

"A block of wood!" said Fool.

"Have a look at this hoof of mine," said the mule.

"I'm looking," said Fool.

"And now pull out one of the nails."

When Fool had drawn a nail out of the hoof, the mule said, "Hammer that nail into the block of wood until you've almost split it!"

And this is just what Fool did. He found the block of wood lying in one corner of the great hall, and drove the nail into it, and the king-in-the-block called out, and begged Fool to spare his life.

Fool spared the king's life, and turned to the princess. "Now you'll marry me," he said.

So Fool and the gold-and-turquoise princess were married. They lived with the old king in the cave palace, and never were three people happier.

"What shall I do now?" said the mule. "Where shall I go?"

"Go home, mule!" said Fool. "Go back to your own field outside my father's palace. You know the way. But," said Fool, "promise you'll come back in seven years, and find out how I'm getting on."

Then Fool thanked the mule for helping him to follow the bird and find the king, and the mule slowly made his way out of the cave on his long journey home.

After seven years, the mule returned to see Fool and the princess and her father. "Will you stable me and feed me?" asked the mule. "I'll serve you and work for you as well as I can."

"You don't have to serve me or work for me," said Fool. "Not when I think of all you did for me, and how you helped me. You'll always be welcome here."

"Then," said the mule, "you see that little bush over there?"

"I'm looking at it," said Fool.

"Uproot it and give me three blows with it."

The moment Fool struck the mule for the third time, the mule was released from the spell that had reined him and ruled him for seven years. And who was he but Fool's own lost father, the king thought to have been drowned in a hinny of a storm?

So Fool and his princess and the two old kings lived together in the cave palace. I visited them myself, and they were all well, wealthy and happy.

THE DAUNTLESS GIRL

"Dang it!" said the farmer.

"Why?" said the miller.

"Not a drop left," the farmer said.

"Not one?" asked the blacksmith, raising his glass and inspecting it. His last inch of whisky glowed like molten honey in the flickering firelight.

"Why not?" said the miller.

"You fool!" said the farmer. "Because the bottle's empty." He peered into the flames. "Never mind that though," he said. "We'll send out my Mary. She'll go down to the inn and bring us another bottle."

"What?" said the blacksmith. "She'll be afraid to go out on such a dark night, all the way down to the village, and all on her own."

"Never!" said the farmer. "She's afraid of nothing – nothing live or dead. She's worth all my lads put together."

The farmer gave a shout and Mary came out of the kitchen. She stood and she listened. She went out into the dark night and in a little time she returned with another bottle of whisky.

The miller and the blacksmith were delighted. They drank to her health, but later the miller said, "That's a strange thing, though."

"What's that?" asked the farmer.

"That she should be so bold, your Mary."

"Bold as brass," said the blacksmith. "Out and alone and the night so dark."

"That's nothing at all," said the farmer. "She'd go anywhere, day or night. She's afraid of nothing – nothing live or dead."

"Words!" said the blacksmith. "But my, this whisky tastes good."

"Words nothing," said the farmer. "I bet you a golden guinea that neither of you can name anything that girl will not do."

The miller scratched his head and the blacksmith peered at the golden guinea of whisky in his glass. "All right," said the blacksmith. "Let's meet here again at the same time next week. Then I'll name something Mary will not do."

Seven days later the blacksmith went to see the priest and borrowed the key of the church door from him. Then he paid a visit to the sexton and showed him the key.

"What do you want with that?" asked the sexton.

"What I want with you," said the blacksmith, "is this. I want you to go into the church tonight, just before midnight, and hide yourself in the dead house."

"Never!" said the sexton.

"Not for half a guinea?" asked the blacksmith.

The old sexton's eyes popped out of his head. "Dang it!" he said. "What's that for then?"

"To frighten that brazen farm girl, Mary," said the blacksmith, grinning. "When she comes to the dead house, just give a moan or a holler."

The old sexton's desire for the half guinea was even greater than his fear. He hummed and hawed and at last he agreed to do as the blacksmith asked. Then the blacksmith clumped the sexton on the back with his massive fist and the old sexton coughed. "I'll see you tomorrow," said the blacksmith, "and settle the account. Just before midnight, then! Not a minute later!"

The sexton nodded and the blacksmith strode up to the farm. Darkness was falling and the farmer and the miller were already drinking and waiting for him.

"Well?" said the farmer.

The blacksmith grasped his glass then raised it and rolled the whisky around his mouth.

"Well," said the farmer. "Are you or aren't you?"

"This," said the blacksmith, "is what your Mary will not do. She won't go into the church alone at midnight…"

"No," said the miller.

"… and go to the dead house," continued the blacksmith, "and bring back a skull bone. That's what she won't do."

"Never," said the miller.

The farmer gave a shout and Mary came out of the kitchen. She stood and she listened; and later, at midnight, she went out into the darkness and walked down to the church.

Mary opened the church door. She held up her lamp and clattered down the steps to the dead house. She pushed open its creaking door and saw skulls and thigh bones and bones of every kind gleaming in front of her. She stooped and picked up the nearest skull bone.

"Let that be!" moaned a muffled voice from behind the dead house door. "That's my mother's skull bone."

So Mary put that skull down and picked up another.

"Let that be!" moaned a muffled voice from behind the dead house door. "That's my father's skull bone."

So Mary put that skull bone down too and picked up yet another one. And, as she did so, she angrily called out, "Father or mother, sister or brother, I *must* have a skull bone and that's my last word." Then she walked out of the dead house, latched the door, and hurried up the steps and back up to the farm.

Mary put the skull bone on the table in front of the farmer. "There's your skull bone, master," she said, and started off for the kitchen.

"Wait a minute!" said the blacksmith, and he was grinning and shivering. "Didn't you hear anything in the dead house, Mary?"

"Yes," she said. "Some fool of a ghost called out: 'Let that be! That's my mother's skull bone' and 'Let that be! That's my father's skull bone.' But I told him straight: 'Father or mother, sister or brother, I *must* have a skull bone.' "

The miller and the blacksmith stared at Mary and shook their heads.

"So I took one," said Mary, "and here it is." She looked down at the three faces flickering in the firelight. "After I had locked the door," she said, "and climbed the steps, I heard the old ghost hollering and shrieking like mad."

At once the blacksmith and the miller got to their feet.

"That'll do then, Mary," said the farmer.

The blacksmith knew the sexton must have been scared out of his wits at being locked inside the dead house. He and his friends hurried down to the church, and clattered down the steps into the dead house. They were too late. They found the old sexton lying stone dead on his face.

"That's what comes to trying to frighten a poor young girl," said the farmer.

So the blacksmith gave the farmer a golden guinea and the farmer gave it to his Mary.

Mary and her daring were known in every house. And after her visit to the dead house, and the death of the old sexton, her fame spread for miles and miles around.

One day the squire, who lived three villages off, rode up to the farm and asked the farmer if he could talk to Mary.

"I've heard," said the squire, "that you're afraid of nothing."

Mary nodded.

"Nothing live or dead," said the farmer proudly.

"Listen then!" said the squire. "Last year my old mother died and was buried. But she will not rest. She keeps coming back into the house, and especially at mealtimes."

Mary stood and listened.

"Sometimes you can see her, sometimes you can't. And when you can't, you can still see a knife and fork get up off the table and play about where her hands would be."

"That's a strange thing altogether," said the farmer.

"Strange and unnatural," said the squire. "And now my servants won't stay with me, not one of them. They're all afraid of her."

The farmer sighed and shook his head. "Hard to come by, good servants," he said.

"So," said the squire, "seeing as she's afraid of nothing, nothing live or dead, I'd like to ask your girl to come and work with me."

Mary was pleased at the prospect of such good employment and, sorry as he was to lose her, the farmer saw there was nothing for it but to let her go.

"I'll come," said the girl. "I'm not afraid of ghosts. But you ought to take account of that in my wages."

"I will," said the squire.

So Mary went back with the squire to be his servant. The first thing she always did was to lay a place for the ghost at table, and she took great care not to let the knife and fork lie criss-cross.

At meals, Mary passed the ghost the meat and vegetables and sauce and gravy. And then she said: "Pepper, madam?" and "Salt, madam?"

The ghost of the squire's mother was pleased enough. So things went on the same from day to day until the squire had to go up to London to settle some legal business.

Next morning Mary was down on her knees, cleaning the parlour grate, when she noticed something thin and glimmering push in through the parlour door, which was just ajar; when it got inside the room, the shape began to swell and open out. It was the old ghost.

For the first time, the ghost spoke to the girl. "Mary," she said in a hollow voice, "are you afraid of me?"

"No, madam," said Mary. "I've no cause to be afraid of you, for you are dead and I'm alive."

For a while the ghost looked at the girl kneeling by the parlour grate. "Mary," she said, "will you come down into the cellar with me? You mustn't bring a light – but I'll shine enough to light the way for you."

So the two of them went down the cellar steps and the ghost shone like an old lantern. When they got to the bottom, they went along a passage, and took a right turn and a left, and then the ghost pointed to some loose tiles in one corner. "Pick up those tiles," she said.

Mary did as she was asked. And underneath the tiles were two bags of gold, a big one and a little one.

The ghost quivered. "Mary," she said, "that big bag is for your master. But that little bag is for you, for you are a dauntless girl and deserve it."

Before Mary could open the bag or even open her mouth, the old ghost drifted up the steps and out of sight. She was never seen again and Mary had a devil of a time groping her way along the dark passage and up out of the cellar.

After three days the squire came back from London.

"Good morning, Mary," he said. "Have you seen anything of my mother while I've been away?"

"Yes, sir," said Mary. "That I have." She opened her eyes wide. "And if you aren't afraid of coming down into the cellar with me, I'll show you something."

The squire laughed. "I'm not afraid if you're not afraid," he said, for the dauntless girl was a very pretty girl.

So Mary lit a candle and led the squire down into the cellar, walked along the passage, took a right turn and a left, and raised the loose tiles in the corner for a second time.

"Two bags," said the squire.

"Two bags of gold," said Mary. "The little one is for you and the big one is for me."

"Lor!" said the squire, and he said nothing else. He did think that his mother might have given him the big bag, as indeed she had, but all the same he took what he could.

After that, Mary always crossed the knives and forks at mealtimes to prevent the old ghost from telling what she had done.

The squire thought things over: the gold and the ghost and Mary's good looks. What with one thing and another he proposed to Mary, and the dauntless girl, she accepted him. In a little while they married, and so the squire did get one hand on the big bag of gold after all.

Boo!

She didn't like it at all when her father had to go down to London and, for the first time, she had to sleep alone in the old house. She went up to her bedroom early. She turned the key and locked the door. She latched the windows and drew the curtains. Then she peered inside her wardrobe, and pulled open the bottom drawer of her clothes press; she got down on her knees and looked under the bed.

She undressed; she put on her nightdress.

She pulled back the heavy linen cover and climbed into bed. Not to read but to try and sleep – she wanted to sleep as soon as she could. She reached out and turned off the lamp.

"That's good," said a little voice. "Now we're safely locked in for the night."

SOURCES OF THE TALES

THE COW THAT ATE THE PIPER

Folktales of Ireland edited and translated by Sean O'Sullivan (1966).

FAIRY OINTMENT

Traditions, Legends, Superstitions, and Sketches of Devonshire, on the Borders of the Tamar and Tavy by Mrs A. E. Bray (1838); *Popular Romances of the West of England* by Robert Hunt (1865); *English Fairy Tales* by Joseph Jacobs (1890).

THE FROG PRINCE

"The Paddo" in *Popular Rhymes of Scotland* by Robert Chambers (1826).

THE SHEPHERD'S TALE

Untitled story in *Cumbrian Superstitions* by W. Howells (1831); *British Goblins* by William Wirt Sikes (1880).

TOM TIT TOT

Ipswich Journal (1878).

BILLY

"The Wee Tailor" in *A Dictionary of British Folk-Tales* by Katharine M. Briggs (1970–1).

THREE HEADS OF THE WELL

Popular Rhymes and Nursery Tales of England by James Orchard Halliwell (-Phillips) (1849).

HUGHBO

"The brownie of Copinsay" in *The Folklore of Orkney and Shetland* by Ernest W. Marwick (1975).

MONDAY, TUESDAY

"The Legend of Knockgrafton" in *Fairy Legends and Traditions from the South of Ireland* by Thomas Crofton Croker (1825).

SAMUEL'S GHOST

"Sammle's Ghost" in "Legends of the Cars" by Mrs M. C. Balfour in *Folk-Lore II* (1891).

THE CHANGELING

The Fairy Mythology by Thomas Keightley (1828).

MOSSYCOAT

Folktales of England edited by Katharine M. Briggs and Ruth L. Tongue (1965).

KING OF THE CATS

More English Fairy Tales by Joseph Jacobs (1894).

DATHERA DAD

Household Tales, with other Traditional Remains by Sydney Oldall Addy (1895).

SEA-WOMAN

"The Mermaid Wife" in *The Fairy Mythology* by Thomas Keightley (1828).

CHARGER

"The Fairy-Chapman" from *The Fairy Mythology* by Thomas Keightley (1828).

THE THREE BLOWS

The Physicians of Myddvai (sic) by Mr Rees of Tonn (1861).

THE MULE

The Kiltartan Wonder Book by Lady Gregory (1910).

THE DAUNTLESS GIRL

The Recreations of a Norfolk Antiquary by Walter Rye (1920).

BOO!

A Dictionary of British Folk-Tales by Katharine M. Briggs (1970–1).